SEYMOUR, THE FORMERLY FEARFUL

EVE B. FELDMAN

KAR-BEN
PUBLISHING

KAR-BEN PUBLISHING
A division of Lerner Publishing Group, Inc.
241 First Avenue North
Minneapolis, MN 55401 USA
1-800-4-KARBEN

Website address: www.karben.com

Cover illustration by Parwinder Singh.

Main body text set in Bembo Std Regular 11.5/16.
Typeface provided by Monotype Typography.

Library of Congress Cataloging-in-Publication Data

Names: Feldman, Eve, author | Singh, Parwinder, illustrator.
Title: Seymour, the formerly fearful / by Eve B. Feldman ; illustrated by Parwinder
    Singh.
Description: Minneapolis : Kar-Ben Publishing, [2019] | Series: Kar-Ben for older
    readers | Originally published: New York : Four Winds Press, 1990. | Summary:
    Fourth-grader Seymour Goldfarb, a confirmed chicken, learns to overcome some of
    his fears when his Israeli cousin, fresh out of the army, comes for the summer.
Identifiers: LCCN 2018012803 (print) | LCCN 2018018834 (ebook) |
    ISBN 9781541542198 (eb pdf) | ISBN 9781541539518 (pb : alk. paper)
Subjects: | CYAC: Fear—Fiction. | Cousins—Fiction. | Jews—United States—
    Fiction. | Self-confidence—Fiction. | Israelis—United States—Fiction. | Camps—
    Fiction.
Classification: LCC PZ7.F33577 (ebook) | LCC PZ7.F33577 Se 2019 (print) | DDC
    [Fic]—dc23

LC record available at https://lccn.loc.gov/2018012803

Manufactured in the United States of America
1-45200-36081-6/5/2018

For my cousin and my friend, Pessach Seidel,
who has made a wonderful difference in my life
and for the five gifts—Sophie, Ethan,
Zach, Jared and Elliott
—E.B.F.

1

KLUTZ

A basketball was coming right at my head, and I threw up my hands in self-defense. "Ow!" I yelled as the ball crunched against my finger. I grabbed my injured hand with my good one. "I think it's broken," I moaned.

"Time-out, time-out," Ted called. It helps when your best friend is captain of the team.

"What's wrong, Seymour?" Everyone was crowding around me.

I tried to act cool. "Ah, nothing. Just a broken finger, probably."

The sound of a shrill whistle announced the approach of Mr. Evans, our gym teacher. "I could have predicted it would be you, Goldfarb," he barked at me. "On the last day of school, too." His muscles rippled as he started writing something down on his clipboard. "What did you do this time?"

I wanted to tell him, "It was dumb to have gym on the last day of school, Mr. Evans, and it was because of this dumb gym class that I got hurt," but I controlled myself and said absolutely nothing. Silently, I showed him my finger, which was starting to swell.

"Someday they'll do a set of X-rays on you and find out why you are such a medical marvel, Goldfarb: a magnet for balls and injuries." Mr. Evans chuckled at his own joke.

"Don't you think he'd better go to the nurse, Mr. Evans?" Ted suggested. Mr. Evans loves Ted as much as he can't stand me.

"Yes, you might as well go, Goldfarb," Mr. Evans agreed.

"Do you want me to go with you?" Ted asked me.

"No, stay and finish the game," I said. "I could probably find the nurse's office blindfolded, and my broken finger won't even make me limp." Everyone but Mr. Evans laughed. Ted slapped me gently on the back.

Mrs. McShane, the school nurse, was busy packing up the last thermometer when I walked in the door. I guess she was not too surprised to see me in her office, even on the very last day of school.

"Oh, it's you, Seymour. What is it?"

I showed her my finger. "Hmm, how'd you do that?" she asked calmly. As she spoke, she opened the little refrigerator that stands in her office and handed me a blue plastic ice pack from the otherwise empty shelves. "Hold this on your finger, Seymour."

I was glad she didn't say something like, "I've been expecting you, Seymour. No day would be complete without our school klutz, would it?" (Klutz is a Yiddish word for an extremely clumsy person.)

After a minute, she took the ice pack off and bent my finger around. "Does this hurt?" she asked.

"Ow! Yes." I winced. You'd think that a person with so much experience in pain would be better at tolerating it.

"I don't think it's broken," Mrs. McShane concluded, "but just to be on the safe side, I'll immobilize it with a splint. Then your parents can decide if they think it needs to be X-rayed." Mrs. McShane knows that my parents are both doctors.

Everyone assumes that my folks can just take care of my many and varied injuries at home. But that's not their specialty. My father always jokes about it: "Sy, if I'd known you were going to be my son, I'd have gone into plastic surgery or orthopedics. I'm no use to you as an ear, nose, and throat specialist."

Mom's no help, either; she's a neurologist. Neurologists take care of heads and spines and serious stuff, though at the rate I'm going, maybe she will get to take care of me someday in the future.

"I don't understand why he's so accident prone," she told my father once when they thought I was out of hearing range.

"So, he's a little klutzy; he'll outgrow it," my father reassured my mother. "It's a phase. He'll turn out fine.

With his genes, he can't help but grow into a fine man, a real mensch." (A mensch is much better than the opposite of a klutz. It's a person who can handle the world and does really good things.)

I'm glad my parents have faith in my automatically having some dramatic transformation, because I sure don't. If I were a tadpole, I'd relax, knowing that I'd turn into a frog. If I were a caterpillar, I'd just wait to turn into a butterfly (or with my luck, a moth). But what does a scaredy-cat, klutzy kid turn into? Probably a nerdy-type adult.

Mrs. McShane had produced a long stick of metal, and she bent it around my finger. Then she wrapped tape around it. Now I had a cool-looking bandage, but every time I looked at it, it just reminded me what a klutz I was.

Slowly I walked back outside, just in time to hear the bell ring. We had an hour left, one hour of school. It seemed to me that every kid in the whole world couldn't wait for school to end and summer to begin—everyone but me. I dreaded summer—it was just more time to be outside to face bugs and sports, two things I did not particularly enjoy.

Why was I the only one who liked to be in school, where it was safe (except for gym days)? I couldn't understand why other kids liked to be outside. Outside, you could get hit by a ball, fall down running, or get stung by some frightening-looking insect.

Maybe, I thought, I was the only one smart enough

to worry about those things. But Ted was pretty smart, too, and he didn't worry about getting hurt or being a loser at sports. Actually, Ted's great at anything that has the word *ball* in it. He's on the traveling soccer team, the all-star baseball team, and the school basketball team.

There was no sport invented yet that I was good at. It was too bad that reading, math, and computers were not considered sports. I guess it was amazing that Ted and I were best friends. That's probably because we'd been friends since nursery school, when we were too young to know that I would turn into a klutz, while he would become an athletic wonder.

Maybe I could have been great at sports and stuff if it weren't for this one minor problem I had: I was afraid. It's hard to explain what I was afraid of, because there were too many things. If I'd made two lists, one that said *THINGS I AM NOT AFRAID OF* and the other one called *THINGS I AM AFRAID OF*, you'd see what I mean. I wasn't afraid of eating, school, reading, drawing, computers, and walking slowly. As for the other list, *THINGS I AM AFRAID OF*, I'd probably never even have had enough paper or enough time to write everything all down, unless I could have done it until infinity.

My parents said most kids were afraid of something, had nightmares and stuff, but I knew that I was different. The bus ride that morning was the perfect example:

everyone in my class, and even the little kids on my bus, had been singing, "No more pencils, no more books, no more teacher's dirty looks," and there was I, hating to say goodbye to the classroom and to Mrs. Fitzgerald. I, Seymour J. Goldfarb—the short kid, the only one with a finger wrapped in metal and a dumb blue ice pack—was miserable.

"What's the matter, Seym?" Ted asked as I entered the classroom. "You don't look too good. Does your finger hurt that badly?"

"No, it's not bad at all. It looks worse than it is." I was determined to act cool. I couldn't admit that the real reason for my mood was the end of the school year. Even Ted would have trouble understanding that.

"This has been one of the best fourth grades I've ever taught," Mrs. Fitzgerald told us just a few minutes before the end of the day. "I'm going to miss you, but I'm sure you'll all have a wonderful summer and terrific vacations."

"Hey, Mrs. Fitzgerald, want to come to the beach today?" David suggested. "Jordan is having a birthday beach party. Practically the whole class is going, except for the girls, of course."

"Thanks, David, but I'm busy this afternoon," she said.

Gee, it was so easy for her, I thought. When I got invited to go someplace like the beach, either I had to go, and worry about what would go wrong, or I had to think of an excuse, fast. I've got to admit that I was pretty good at excuses. In fact, I didn't think anyone knew what a scaredy-cat I really was. They just thought I was clumsy. So when I said I had a pulled muscle, a sore tendon, a fractured toe, a trick knee, or a sprained ankle, everyone believed me. That type of injury is hard to prove, so most people just had to take my word for it.

I'd gotten so good at excuses that no one knew that I couldn't ride a two-wheeler. And in my neighborhood, where most guys my age are attached to the seats of their bikes, that was pretty amazing. But I'd worked out a pretty elaborate scheme to keep everyone from figuring out why I didn't ride. If someone said, "Hey, Seymour, do you want to go for a bike ride?," I just said that one of my tires was flat and my parents were too busy working to have it fixed. Everyone knew that they were doctors and that doctors are busy. If anyone offered to lend me a bike, I just said it was too big for me (which it usually was), or I fell back on one of my hard-to-prove ailments.

This time, I had a visible excuse. Mrs. McShane had said to keep my finger dry. That was a perfect last-minute reason to skip Jordan's beach party. As we walked out of school, I felt a little better. I even thought this finger might come in handy after all.

2

A GREAT SOLUTION

My finger was only sprained, and my parents pooh-poohed it.

"It will be better in no time," my father the optimist pronounced. "It certainly won't ruin your summer. You'll be fine for camp."

At the mention of camp, I started worrying again. A klutz should not go to camp. A klutz should probably not go anywhere, but definitely not camp. Even computer camp, which is where I was going.

Life would be so much simpler if I weren't a klutz. I thought about it the whole afternoon while Ted and all the guys were out having fun at Jordan's party. Sitting in front of my computer, in the middle of a great computer game, I started imagining all the guys at the beach party. I could just picture them running merrily, eagerly, into the choppy waves. I was glad I wasn't there, but I wanted to want to be there. Why was I such a wimp? Ted, Jordan, David, and Michael—they were all normal, brave kids. What was wrong with me, Seymour J. Goldfarb?

Suddenly, I knew the answer! It came to me in a

flash—just like that funny saying about a light going on over your head. It was so obvious that I don't know why I hadn't realized it before! It was my name. Seymour is not the name of an athletic captain-of-the-football-team type. And my dad's nickname for me, Sy, was no better. It just sounded as if he was heaving a big sigh whenever he talked to me.

I started chuckling to myself. The solution was so simple—I'd just change my name. I was so excited; I couldn't wait to tell my parents. They'd surely be overjoyed to know that I'd figured out a way to become normal, uninjurable, and unafraid. Why hadn't I thought of it before?

All I had to do was break it to Mom, carefully, gently, at just the right moment. I waited patiently for her to come home from work. Two minutes after she came home seemed to be the perfect time. Mom had plenty of time to walk in and take off her shoes and turn off her work phone. She seemed to be in a pretty good mood, so I told her.

"Mom, I've been thinking about changing my name." She was leafing through the day's mail and made no comment. "I mean it. Mom. I'm going to change my name. Which do you like best, Stuart, Stanley, Seth, or Scott?"

She looked up suddenly. "What's wrong with the name Seymour?"

"It's a twerpy, nerdy name, that's what! Why'd you have to go and give me a name that would ruin my whole life?"

"Seymour, don't be ridiculous. What's gotten into you? Seymour is a beautiful name, and you know why we called you that. It was for my father. It was his name, and he was certainly no twerp. He was the handsomest, strongest, most wonderful man I've ever known—not counting your father, of course. And it's a beautiful Jewish tradition to name your child after a beloved deceased relative, you know that!"

"Mom, we learned about names in Hebrew school, and I'm the only kid with such a weird name. All the other kids who are named after their relatives just used the first initial. Michael is named after his grandfather Menachem, but that's only his Hebrew name. His folks didn't call him Menachem! Ted is named for someone named Tessie. His parents didn't call him Tessie! And Jordan, yeah, Jordan is named for an uncle who was called Yehekziel, and Yechie was his nickname. His parents didn't call him Yechie! They realized what a bad name could do to a person." I paused to take a breath. Mom was eyeing me doubtfully. "But don't worry, Mom, I understand what this means to you," I went on. "That's why, when I change my name, in memory of your father, I would keep the *S* and just change it to Stanley or Stuart, Steven, Sam,

Scott, or Seth. There's a whole bunch of normal choices." I didn't even mention the lucky kids at school, like Carlos and Richard, who weren't named after anyone.

My mother sighed. "If you'd only known your grandfather, you'd be proud to have his name. This is sheer nonsense, Seymour. You'll grow into your name; you'll grow into a fine young man. Now I don't want to hear any more of this nonsense. Topic closed."

My mother may be short and thin and quiet most of the time, but when she says things like "topic closed," and she puts her hands on her hips and her eyes start to flash, she means business.

Well, maybe the topic was closed for her, but it wasn't for me. What did my parents know about having to live with an awful name? My mother's name is Judy and my father's is David, two regular, average, non-nerdy names. How would Mom know what a mushy name could do to a kid? I bet they would have called me Yechie if that had been my grandfather's name! Yuch!

Despite my mother's opinion, I still thought that Seymour was a twerpy name. If I didn't get rid of it, I knew I was going to have to find an even more drastic solution. I needed a total makeover.

I won't even tell you my middle name. I've never told anyone my middle name, and I don't think I ever will unless I get tortured. I'm not too great about torture.

3

OH NO, OH NO,
IT'S OFF TO CAMP I GO

I thought I'd planned the summer carefully enough not to have to worry about my fears. I was going to computer camp. It wasn't a sleepaway camp. Ted went to a sleepaway camp, and he tried to convince me to go with him.

"Seymour, you should see the video from Camp Sportahana."

With a name like that, I already knew it couldn't be for me.

"What kind of name is that for a camp?"

"It sounds Indian, doesn't it?"

"Not to me." To me it sounded just awful, but Ted kept begging me to see it and his parents talked to my parents, so I had to at least sit through the video.

They all thought the camp looked terrific. It had every kind of sport imaginable and ones I'd never even heard of before, like pool polo and squash—definitely not my style.

"What do you think of that camp, Sy?" my father asked when the video ended.

"Uh, it seems terrific, but I am really heavily engrossed in a program that I am writing on my computer and I just thought that computer camp would be more relevant to me." (I knew that if I threw in enough impressive-sounding words, they would take me more seriously.)

My father smiled proudly. He enjoys the fact that I'm smart, so somehow that ended that. I was still worried that my parents would try to send me to a sleep-away computer camp, so I prepared a thousand arguments against going away, but they never suggested it.

There was barely any time between the end of school and the start of camp, so I was starting to think that this year maybe I'd be lucky. I mean I figured there'd be no time for the kids to get a mother to take us all to the beach or the pool, and it was too hot to get into ball games and other horrors at the park. Besides, most of the guys my age were going away to camp and they left even before my camp started. And there was always my injured finger to keep me from doing all the things I hated doing.

So on the day before my camp was going to start, I was not as nervous and worried as I usually was about new things. Besides, I kept telling myself, every time my stomach did get that sort of shaky feeling I got when I was really scared, what could there be at a computer day camp to worry me?

By the time the bus came the next morning, I was ready—ready with a whole list of things to worry about:

What if everyone on the bus knew everyone else on the bus and I was the only one who knew no one?

What if the bus was so late getting to camp that everyone had already gone to the activities?

What if we got to camp, and all the kids knew where they were supposed to go except for me?

What if we got to camp, and the director or head counselor called off everyone's name from a long list and my name wasn't on it?

What if the ride was very long and I had to go to the bathroom before we got there?

What if everyone knew more about computers than I did?

What if my group was all girls except for me?

What if I left my camp bag on the bus with my camp hat and bathing suit and stuff?

What if we all had to change into bathing suits in one big room and the other guys were awful?

What if lunch was spinach pie or gizzard stew with stewed rhubarb for dessert?

What if I got on the wrong bus on the way home?

What if no one was home when I got home and I forgot my key?

These are just a few of the problems that crossed my mind. The amazing thing is that I hadn't ever even considered what turned out to be the real problems.

First of all, my finger was healed by the time camp started—no more swelling, no more bluish-purplish color, no more cute metal bandage to protect me from sports.

The next problem was that even though this was a computer camp, we didn't work with computers all day. Mornings were for computers, but that still left a whole afternoon to be terrified about. Two days we could pick activities for part of the afternoon, so of course I picked arts and crafts, but then the choices left were awful. Besides the usual sports like basketball and tennis, they had drama (I was afraid to go onstage); nature (with bugs and snakes and all that gross stuff); hiking (not much of an improvement on nature); and woodworking (I was sure I'd cut off at least a few fingers, if not a total hand or maybe a foot or a foot and a hand). But the other alternatives were so bad that I actually chose woodworking. I just tried to avoid the saw, the hammer, and the nails.

In fact, I spent a great deal of time sanding, until the woodworking instructor even noticed. He said, "Seymour, if you sand any more, you'll have nothing left of that boat but wood chips."

"I just want it to be really smooth," I explained.

"It's so smooth, it's slippery. Paint it already, and start on something else."

So I painted it, very slowly of course, using the thinnest brush I could find. That helped.

Meanwhile, on the other three days, we had regularly scheduled activities, no choices. So I had to start a new bruise collection as we played all the sports imaginable from *a* to *v*: aerobics to volleyball. Volleyball wasn't too bad except when it was my turn to serve, but aerobics was the pits, because it was coed. Ugh!

And who else do you think went to computer camp and ended up in my coed aerobics? Lari Blume. No, I didn't misspell it. Lari is a girl's spelling for Larry, and Lari Blume is definitely a girl. I mean, not only is she a girl, but she is a *girl*! Big blue eyes, long blond hair, and dimples. We went to the same school, and she'd never been in my class, but I knew who she was. Who wouldn't? Well, it was mortifying to have to do aerobics with her. I was sure that sooner or later I'd crash into her or accidentally trip her or something. I really didn't have to worry about that, though, because it happened right away. The second day of camp, I crashed into her. Only it wasn't aerobics; it was lunch.

I slipped in the lunchroom (though no banana peels or wax were visible), and I slid across the floor, landing smack on Lari. Somehow I didn't spill the entire contents of my cup during the slide over. No, just my luck, there was enough left in the cup to land all over Lari.

"Ooo, ick!" shrieked this blond goddess as she tried to clean the mess off her cute pink T-shirt and her shining tan arms.

Her friends were more blunt.

"What's your problem, wimp?" someone said, and they all laughed. I muttered something like "I'm sorry" and tried to disappear.

The second day and I'd already struck out, without even needing a bat and a ball to do it.

4
OVER MY HEAD

As a fearful person, I've learned that there are words for people who are afraid of things: *phobia* is a fancy name for "fears," and *phobic* is "fearful." Then you can put another weird-sounding word in front of it (prefix, I think it's called), and you will know what a person is afraid of. Like fear of heights is acrophobia, and fear of water is aquaphobia.

Now, despite all the things I have been telling you about myself, I was not an aquaphobic. I was not afraid of water. I'll prove it. I drank water, I loved to take showers and baths, and I would cross a puddle if, of course, I was wearing boots. So I wasn't an aquaphobic, right? Wrong.

I wasn't afraid of water in a glass or a bathtub or a puddle, but I wasn't too thrilled about water in a pool or an ocean. I'd read somewhere that it was possible to drown in just an inch of water. If it could be done, I could probably do it.

Well, I'd been to pools before, and I wasn't completely scared. As long as I could keep my feet on the ground and my head out of the water, I was fine. I could even move through the water, with a nice, easy stroke also known as the dog paddle. But I wouldn't even do that in a place where I couldn't stand if necessary.

I never imagined that there was a pool built for giants, but, trust me, I have now seen one. My computer camp was on the grounds of a college, so we had to use the college pool. The college pool's lowest point was over my nostrils, which isn't, I suppose, as bad as if it were all the way over my hair, but it was close enough to be just as bad. And they actually expected me to get in that thing!

Calmly, with only a little tiny quiver in my voice, I explained first to my counselor and then to the swimming counselor that I was allergic to chlorine.

"I mean, I can go swimming if I don't get my head wet, I mean, if I don't swallow the water or anything like that," I told them.

"Bring a note." The swimming instructor barely looked at me while he shouted instructions to someone else. "For today, I guess you'd better sit it out."

"Don't worry, Seymour," my counselor said soothingly. "Rich is a great swimming instructor, and I'm sure he'll figure out what to do. You won't have to miss swimming."

Who, me, worry?

The other kids were all in the water, splashing and splashing, not thinking about drowning or getting chlorine down their throats.

That night, after dinner, I approached my mom for a note. My father is usually tougher, although they both understand about me and chlorine because they've seen me spit and spatter and cough and feel awful from it. Mom is a firm believer in allergies anyway, since she has a few herself.

"Mom, this pool at camp is like for college-age people and it's like seventeen thousand feet deep and five miles long so they must have put several million gallons of chlorine in it to keep it filtered and you know how I get around chlorine . . ."

"Well, I never thought the pool would be so deep. It sounds like an Olympic-sized pool." Mom sounded as concerned as I was, almost.

"What's this about the pool?" Dad asked, entering the kitchen and the conversation at the same time.

Mom explained the problem, and he calmly reassured me. "Seymour, if you just swim and keep your mouth closed, it shouldn't matter how deep it is. Besides, maybe you've outgrown that allergy thing." He looked at me closely.

"David, I am going to write him a note." Mom looked at Dad and then added, "But I'm sure, Seymour, that they'll find a way for you to swim."

Yeah, I thought, with a gas mask and a life preserver I'll consider it.

Of course they all won out in the end. Rich read my mom's note. "Okay, Seymour, no problem," he said. I figured that meant that I was excused from swimming, so I started to walk away. "Wait a minute, Seymour, where are you going?"

"Well, you read the note, so I thought I'd go sit over there and watch," I volunteered.

"No watching when I'm around!" he boomed. I started wondering if he might be related to Mr. Evans, my non-favorite gym teacher. "Listen, you'll just tread water and swim or hold on to the wall except during instruction. And I'll see to it that you're not required to do things where you need to keep your head under water, like the dead man's float."

If I hadn't been terrified, I might have laughed at the "dead man's float."

I did what Rich said, not happily, but I did it. I looked at the other kids. No one else seemed upset. No one else seemed to be bothered by the size and depth of this pool. Maybe that's because no one in camp was younger than me and I'm really short for my age, so everyone else could touch bottom. The only other kid who looked anywhere near as miserable as me was Kevin. Everyone called him Kevin the Blob, so as you can imagine, he wasn't too thrilled even being in a bathing suit. When Kevin sat down, he looked as if he had an extra stomach on top of his regular one.

Kevin wanted to be my friend. He wasn't too eager to play all those sports, either, so he signed up for a few of the same specialties that I did. I didn't call him Blob or anything, but I didn't really like him, either, because he never laughed and all he talked about was food. Before lunch he'd say, "Wonder what we are having for lunch?" After lunch he'd say, "Wonder what we are having for lunch tomorrow?"

I tried not thinking about lunch. I had enough to worry about between Lari and swimming and sports. Lunch, I learned fast, was either all right because you could tell what it was or terrible because you could tell what it was, but it wasn't the way it should have been. Like macaroni and cheese. I like macaroni and cheese, but not macaroni and cheese à la computer camp. This stuff was made of all different-colored noodles and had vegetables in it too. I thought about going to peek in the kitchen to see the chef. I figured he must be one weird guy. I imagined him looking like an alien from one of the computer games. And I pictured him standing with a cookbook called *How to Ruin Food That Kids Used to Like*. When we had hot dogs that curled up and the ends met in the middle, I decided that the chef might even have written the cookbook himself! So I really didn't feel like making it worse by hanging out with Kevin.

5
COLOR OF WAR

Just when I thought things at camp couldn't get worse, they did. The director, Dr. Harris, called us all together and announced that this year, for the first time, they were going to have Color War at computer camp. Just my luck. Color War is when the whole camp divides into different colors and everyone competes as teammates. Color War is what I'd always dreaded at the awful little day camps I used to go to. Color War was one of the things I had planned to miss by choosing a computer camp.

The director divided us into four color groups: Green, Blue, Yellow, and Orange. As he was finishing calling off our names, I suddenly had a brainstorm, a way to waste some time. I raised my hand and called out at the same time, "How about naming our teams?"

The other kids liked that idea. They all started cheering, and everyone was talking at once. Dr. Harris had to blow his whistle and shout in his megaphone a few times before order was restored. He agreed to allow names, as long as they were computer-related. Most people seemed to think that was an idea we could live with, although there were a few boos in the crowd.

People started arguing about what sort of names to pick.

Should we use names of computer games like Ork and Swampcatcher? Or names of computer parts, like Keyboard and Monitor and Disk Drive and Printer? Or just computer-related words like RAM and Byte and Memory and Font? (That was my idea.) This discussion was terrific because it wasted a great deal of Color War time. I'm not sure that Dr. Harris appreciated it as much as I did, though. He really blasted that whistle.

"Well, campers, that was quite a lively discussion and very appropriate for our camp. It shows that you are learning a lot about computers here. However, we are spending a good amount of precious Color War time arguing, so I have reached a decision. The teams will be Keyboards, Cables, Monitors, and Printers." He paused. I think he was waiting for a cheer, but there weren't any, so he assigned each color group a team name.

Lari's team was Keyboards. And my team was Cables, the most boring part of a computer.

"During Color War, you must wear a shirt the same color as the color of your team," Dr. Harris concluded, beaming.

The choices were gross, and of course, I got the grossest, Orange. I owned one orange shirt that was a hand-me-down from some cousin so long ago that I could barely remember his name or his face. So, of course, this shirt was not exactly high style.

I knew I'd have to wash out this putrid shirt every night and stick it in the dryer. If I left it for my mom, she might forget, and then I'd get mixed up with one of the other teams and they'd all kill me.

The next day Color War officially started. The only part that I had a chance at being good at was a computer maze race, which I managed to win for my team. Unfortunately, Lari was my competitor on the Yellow team, so even though I won, it meant beating her, which was still another reason for her to hate me. And she looked good in yellow and would have looked good in blue or orange or green too.

As for all the other contests, you can imagine how a klutz would do in a relay race or in any of the normal baseball and soccer games and all. Even in the stuff that required no special physical talent, I managed to foul up royally. Like in one part, we all had to throw our sneakers into a huge pile and then when the whistle blew we were supposed to dive in and retrieve our own sneakers and get them on fast. Sounds easy, except my sneakers were so tight that I knew I'd be the last one finished, or close to it. (Kevin was the last.) When they first described the rules of this contest, I raised my hand and asked if kids with Velcro instead of shoelaces would be excused. (I would have managed to dig up a pair of Velcro sneakers somewhere.) But everyone said that it wouldn't be fair to disqualify people just because they had Velcro sneakers and then someone else suggested counting how many people on each team had Velcro and then redividing everyone to be sure there were the same number of Velcro sneakers on every team. Then someone else said what about just making a rule that you didn't have to tie any sneakers. Then the director said we couldn't do that because people could trip and sue the camp. At least my one little question killed quite a bit more of Color War time.

When the whole ordeal was finally over, Lari's team won. I could have predicted that from day one. Anyone with a cool name like Lari and who looks like Lari is a natural winner. My team came in third, which wasn't as bad as it could have been, I guess. We could have been fourth. I felt bad that I hadn't been much help, but I was thrilled that it was finally over.

The only good thing that happened was that when Color War was over, everyone started tearing up his or her shirts. While I didn't have the nerve to rip mine, some of the guys in my group got bored when they finished tearing their shirts. So they just grabbed for mine as I changed for afternoon swim. I didn't stop them. Now I had the perfect excuse for throwing out that disgusting orange shirt.

6

MY PARENTS' SURPRISE

It was the last week of camp when my mom and dad came into my room with a letter and some "good news." The letter was from my mom's cousin Ruth. I'd heard about Ruth, but I'd never actually seen her, because she lives in Israel. Ruth's father and my mother's father were first cousins, but my grandfather's family came to this country from Europe, and Ruth's father's family went to live in Israel. My parents have seen Ruth because they went to Israel right after they got married, and Ruth was here once, too, but I was a baby then. So I didn't even know her!

Well, my parents were all excited because Ruth's son, who I guess is sort of my cousin too, was coming for a visit.

"Sy," cooed my mother, "isn't that wonderful?"

"What's so wonderful about it? How long is he coming for?"

She either didn't hear or just ignored my first question.

"Let me see." She reread the letter quickly. "Six weeks."

"Six weeks?" I tried not to shriek, but I'm not sure I succeeded. "You mean I have to take care of this Israeli kid for six weeks?"

They both laughed. "He's not exactly a kid, and you certainly don't have to take care of him. But we did think you'd enjoy having an older boy around for a few weeks."

I looked at my parents as if they had just dropped in from Planet Mars. Why would any normal person want to have an older boy around, even for a few weeks? Ted has an older brother, so I know about this from firsthand experience. Ted's brother is always screaming at him, tricking him, sending him on stupid errands, annoying us, and interrupting our games. Why would my parents think I'd want someone like that around for even two seconds?

"Why does he have to stay with us?" I had to ask.

"Seymour, I can't believe you could be that ungracious and selfish. What is wrong with you?" my father bellowed at me.

I felt tears stinging my eyes. I'd survived Color War for this?

My mother put her hand on my head. "Stop yelling at him, David. It's just that he hasn't had time to think about it. I'm sure when he has, Seymour will realize what fun it's going to be. And besides, it's already been decided. In fact, he'll be arriving next week."

Next week was too soon for me. Even never was too soon for me.

But of course, he came, two days before the end of camp. I hadn't been looking forward to meeting him, but when he came, I was so out of it, I forgot to be upset.

He came the night of the day we had a computer camp first: an end-of-camp boat trip to the Statue of Liberty. Why did they have to try out all their firsts on me? I don't like being a guinea pig.

I should have thought of a way to stay home that day, but I was so busy worrying about the arrival of my Israeli cousin that I forgot it was the day of the boat ride.

So I ended up on a bus to New York City, and the next thing, I was stepping onto a huge sailboat with enormous sails. I think they called it a tall ship, and I'd even seen one on TV. But on TV, you couldn't tell if the passengers were petrified or what. If they'd had a TV camera on me, you'd have been able to tell that I was scared, even if it were shot long-distance. I was sure that I'd be the one person who fell into the water just stepping onto the boat. But both my feet actually made it over the gap between the dock and the boat. I kept telling myself that everything would be fine, but I can tell when I am lying to myself. There were three groups of kids, one my age and two older ones. I kept wishing I were younger—too young to be at this camp and on this boat.

I tried to look calm and normal, and I think I succeeded for about two seconds. That's when I realized something was wrong. It was incredibly windy, the waves were lapping against the boat, and all of a sudden a gust of wind appeared and half the boat was drenched with water spray or something. All the kids and the counselors on the boat laughed. Except me. I thought I'd die. I forgot all about my Israeli cousin and all other major problems and concentrated on the problem at hand: surviving. One of the counselors was throwing up over the side of the boat. She was facing the wind and, whammo, the wind blew it back all over her and a few other people. The other kids shrieked, but they shrieked because it was gross but fun. I was too speechless to shriek.

The boat started tipping. We were traveling on our side. I stroked my life vest for comfort. Some of the kids went downstairs and came up laughing, saying they couldn't keep their balance down there. Downstairs there was a kitchen and a bathroom, called The Head. During the first big dip, the door had blown open and broken. I prayed I wouldn't need the bathroom for a few hours . . .

I sat on a bench by the wheel that steers the boat. It seemed like the only spot where you could sit and hold on to something without sliding around. I watched the young guy who was steering the boat. He looked about the same age as my counselor—young, very young. The crew were two guys and three girls, who were probably gorgeous, but I was too terrified to look closely. The counselors were talking to them, so they seemed too busy to notice how bad it was. I asked one of the crew girls if this was normal sailing.

"Well, it is a bit rough, but we don't have to worry with such a wonderful captain." She smiled.

"Where is the captain?" I asked. Maybe he was down below, radioing for help or something.

She looked at me as if I were crazy. "He's right in front of you!" she said, pointing at the kid who was steering the wheel.

"He's the captain?" I asked, and my voice sounded shaky.

"Yes," she said, as if she were talking to a moron.

I couldn't believe it. The captain probably weighed less than Kevin, and he must have just graduated from nursery school. What kind of experience could he have had? He couldn't say in a big, booming, reassuring voice, "In my fifty years at sea, I've weathered much worse weather than this." He couldn't even say that in a little squeaky voice.

I looked at the captain and the crew. I watched them as they tried to move the sails. They had to ask for help from all the adults on the boat, and even Kevin, to fight that tough wind. It did not look good. In fact, it looked bad.

One of the girl counselors came and sat next to me.

"You don't look like you're having too much fun," she said.

I couldn't think of a good reply, so I said nothing.

"Is this your first trip sailing?" she continued.

"First and last." I tried to sound as if I were joking.

She smiled. "Don't worry," she said calmly, "I've sailed a lot, and this isn't so bad. Only when the water is all white and foamy is it *really* bad."

We both glanced at the water. It was so white and foamy that it looked as if somebody had spilled bubble bath in it, the huge ocean-sized bottle variety.

But she didn't seem worried. "I've seen worse," she said as she got up and rolled from side to side with the boat. I was beginning to think that I was crazy. No one else looked worried. Kevin came over with a dish piled full of food, and he managed to eat more than half before it got knocked into the sea.

"I'll go get more," he said, just as if nothing unusual had happened. He turned and went toward the downstairs. "Want any?"

I shook my head. I wasn't nauseous or anything, but I wasn't hungry, either. I needed all my energy to concentrate on my terror. The only thing that bothered me was that no one else seemed even mildly disturbed. I decided right then that there are two types of people in this world: the kind who love roller coasters and the kind who hate roller coasters. I figured that somehow I had gotten mixed up with a group where I was the only non-roller coaster fan in the bunch.

The day went by slowly. I had time to think about Christopher Columbus and Leif Eriksson and all the other explorers who had ventured out to sea and been there for days, weeks, and months. I gained real respect for their courage and daring. I wasn't sure I'd survive another few hours. I couldn't imagine being an explorer myself. I thought of the immigrants who had made it by boat to these same waters, and my heart went out to them too. In fact, when we finally turned around and I saw the Statue of Liberty coming up in the right direction—land, land, land—I felt such hope and joy that I could really identify with them.

"Give me liberty from this boat and these waters," I prayed silently, all the way to shore.

I was even jolly on the bus ride back to camp. I was just so overjoyed to be alive. All the other kids were jolly, too, but for the opposite reason—they'd had a great time.

By the time I got home, I'd totally forgotten about my Israeli cousin. I couldn't wait to tell my parents about the boat ride and how I'd managed to survive.

I started slowly, ready to build up to the exciting parts. "You have to hear about the trip I had today."

"Quick, Seymour, take a fast shower," my mother blurted out as she put some soda in the refrigerator.

Soda in our house means company, because my parents are kind of health conscious, but they buy soda and other "junk food" items for guests. Strange, I've always thought—why would you consider it being a good host to give your company something you don't think is good for you? But I happen to like that stuff myself. So I went for the soda.

"Seymour, no time for that now, and you know I don't like it when you drink that stuff. Go take a shower."

"You heard your mother," my father added as he threw some spices into a bubbling pot. (My father loves to cook, and he believes the spicier, the tastier.)

"What's going on here? I just walked in, barely alive after nearly being killed today, and you two start yelling at me." I tried not to raise my voice.

They both glanced up at me but ignored my mention of danger and distress.

"Seymour, we have to go to the airport. Your cousin's plane is coming in, and we want to be sure to be there on time," my mother explained in an exasperated tone.

"Oh, no," I muttered under my breath. "Just what I need. I barely survive drowning, and now I'm supposed to play host to some Israeli kid." But I delivered this speech in mumbles and grunts as I left for the shower.

There was no point in letting them know how I felt. They didn't seem to care about me at all.

I dawdled through the shower, and when my father came in with a "Hurry up, Seymour," I suggested that they go ahead without me.

"I'll wait here and mind the fort while you go get him. I can straighten up the house and stuff."

My father gave me a strange look.

"Get dressed. We're leaving in ten minutes."

7

SHALOM, BEN-DODI

I didn't say a word to my parents all the way to the airport. I wasn't going to give them the satisfaction of hearing about my boat adventure since they hadn't had the decency or curiosity to be interested in the traumatic adventure of their one and only son.

Unbelievably, they seemed to have forgotten that I even existed. As we pulled into Kennedy Airport, they were busy following signs looking for El Al or International Arrivals or whatever. I wasn't paying much attention. If they weren't interested in me, then I certainly wasn't interested in them.

I didn't mind looking at the planes, but I was getting angrier by the minute. They didn't even notice.

My father dropped me and my mom off at the terminal, and he went to park the car. When we walked into the terminal, I almost forgot to be angry, because it was crazy in there. There were people of every size, shape, color, and nationality, and they were all rushing around with suitcases and babies and stuff, and many of them weren't even speaking English. It suddenly occurred to me that it might be hard to find this cousin that nobody really knew. I was glad it wasn't me who was traveling all alone to a strange country. I would have been terrified to walk around among all these people, trying to guess which ones were my family.

"How are we going to find him?" I asked.

"Huh? Come this way. Oh dear, the plane has already landed."

My mom yanked me, and we went flying over to an area that said NO ENTRANCE BEYOND THIS POINT. People were pressed up against a rope barrier, straining to see other people who I guessed were passengers coming off different flights. My mother still hadn't answered my question. Now I was starting to worry about how we'd ever find my father among all these people. I hoped Mom had money for taxi fare in case we lost track of him. As for finding the kid, that seemed like a real mission impossible. I decided I'd at least better keep an eye on my mom. I didn't feel like getting stranded in the airport.

People started coming out of the doors. And what a variety of people! Men in long black coats, with long sideburns (Hassidim, a special kind of religious Jew), young couples with babies, teenagers with backpacks, and a few old couples. And nearly everyone had someone to meet him, as you could tell from the screams of "Danny, over here!" Or "There she is!" People were embracing and crying and jumping around. It was wild. My mother kept pushing on her glasses and looking at the arriving passengers.

"What could be taking your father so long?" she asked me. I didn't see what help he could be, and I told her so.

"But he has the sign."

"What sign?"

"The one with our cousin's name on it, so he'll know we're here for him."

"What is his name, anyway?"

"Pesach, Pesach Raviv."

I kept an eye on all the kids who were coming out of the exit, and all of them were with families. Maybe my cousin was lost already or hadn't ever gotten on the plane. I suggested these two likelihoods to my mother, who looked at me as if I'd just arrived from outer space. She was waving frantically, and I almost thought she'd found my cousin when I realized she was waving at my father.

"Where's the sign?" she hollered.

My father hit his head in exasperation.

"I left it home."

"Now what?" asked my mother.

I was almost glad they were suffering, a punishment

for not paying attention to my misery when I came home from camp.

"We'll find him. Just relax," my father said, but he didn't sound too convinced himself.

I was distracted by all the varieties of luggage that people were carrying: fancy suitcases, plastic bags, cartons tied with string, suitcases tied with belts. Some of the boxes and suitcases had stickers on them about their flight. I was casually glancing at one of those stickers when I saw a tag reading "Pesach Raviv."

"I found him!" I shrieked, dashing toward the suitcase, but the suitcase was standing by itself. My parents turned and followed me.

"Seymour, stay here. You'll get lost. We don't need to look for you too," my mother complained. But my father saw that I was pointing at the suitcase.

He rushed over. "Good work, son. Thank goodness you've found him. Now, where can he be?"

I looked around, but I didn't see any boys without families.

Just then a tall man with dark curly hair and brown sandals came over and went to pick up the suitcase. "I'm sorry," I said. "This belongs to someone."

He looked at me and said, "You are Goldfarb, yes?"

"Pesach!" my parents screeched as they hugged this tall stranger.

Now I was really confused. If this was a kid, he was definitely a giant kid.

"What is your name, *ben-dodi*?" asked the giant. He was talking to me.

"Seymour. How old are you, and what is *ben-dodi*?"

"*Ben-dodi* is 'cousin.' And my age is still not old."

I tugged at my father's sleeve and whispered, "I thought he was a kid. How old is he?" But once again I seemed to be invisible. I, who had nearly drowned on a boat, who had managed to find this cousin who was not a kid, I, their only son, was practically left at the airport. I think if they hadn't used me to help carry some plastic bag, they'd have actually managed to forget me there.

So when we finally got into the car, you can understand that I wasn't in the greatest of moods. I sat in the back with Pesach. My parents were chattering away with him about this relative and that relative, all names with no faces for me. I leaned against the window and would probably have fallen asleep if I hadn't felt a lump of annoyance swelling in my stomach.

I was so busy being resentful that it took me a while to realize that Pesach was asking me something.

"What?" I said, despite myself.

"Is it far from here, your house?"

I looked out the window. I wasn't sure where we were exactly. It was dark, and I was tired and angry.

"Uh, I guess not. We don't live too far from the airport, so it can't be far."

He gave me a funny look and smiled.

"In Israel we learn to know every place carefully, so that we could find our way from anywhere. Maybe I will teach you a little."

Oh, great, I thought, all I need is this guy who's going to brag about how everything is better in Israel.

I excused myself and went to bed as soon as we got home. "Sorry, but I've had a long day," I murmured.

8

TOUR GUIDE

The next morning when I left for camp, Pesach was still sleeping, and I was glad I didn't have to see him. My mother acted as if everything were normal. I just glared at her over my cold cereal.

The last day of camp wasn't too bad. At least I knew my suffering was over, and I wasn't looking forward to being home with my cousin. Even talking about lunch with Kevin seemed better than staying home with this tall stranger.

Some of the groups put on skits as part of a farewell. Lari was in one skit. She wasn't the star or anything, but I kept looking at her instead of at the girl who was the star. My group put on a little skit, too, and I came out carrying a huge computer drawing that we'd made. Everyone cheered. It was really a good drawing, and I didn't even get tangled up in the paper and trip and tear it or anything. Well, only the corner got mushed from my sweaty hands. My hands are always sweaty.

When I stepped off the camp bus, I almost wished it wasn't the last time. Funny how things look good when they're over.

Pesach was in the living room.

"Hi, *ben-dodi*."

"Hi. Why do you call me that?"

"What is your real name? No, don't tell me. I will remember. See, Seem, Simon?"

"No." (But I thought, *Even Simon might be a better name*.) "It's Seymour."

"So I shall call you Seymour?"

"You don't have to."

"Your name in Hebrew, you know it?"

"It is, uh, Shmuel."

"No, Shmuel is Hebrew for Seymour?"

I explained to him how our rabbi had explained to us that in America, people sometimes took liberties in naming their children and didn't translate Hebrew names exactly into English and vice versa. Every Jewish kid is supposed to have a Hebrew name and an English name, and while they are supposed to be the same name, a lot of times they are not.

"Hmm," replied my cousin. "I see I have much to learn about American Jews. But maybe we will find you a better Hebrew name."

"I wouldn't mind a better English name, either," I admitted.

"Seymour is not a good English name?"

I tried to explain about twerps and nerds and how

a name could sound awful and almost make you awful.

Pesach smiled. "We also have names that people, how you say, laugh about, or children do not like to have."

"Like what?" I asked.

"Like Pesach." He laughed. "Do you know what Pesach means?"

"Yeah, it's the Hebrew word for Passover."

"Right. It is not what I would choose for a name. Would you like to be called for a holiday, like Thanksgiving?"

"No way!" I agreed.

"But I do not change my name. I like to be against it, to be different than the name suggests. You know?"

I thought about that for a moment. *Well, if nothing else, we have weird names in common*, I told myself.

"Oh, I almost forgot. You have message." Pesach gestured toward a pad by the phone. It said "Ted."

"Great!" I shrieked. "Ted's my best friend, and he was at sleepaway camp." I had to explain sleepaway camp while I dialed Ted's number. I talked a minute to his mom and then hung up. I felt like a balloon after the air goes out, and I guess it must have showed.

"Ted is not home?"

"No, uh, he went to the park with some of the guys."

"Great, we go too. I want to see American park.

I did not come here to sleep all day. You be my *madrich*, my 'guide.'"

"Uh, nah, I don't feel like the park. I've had a long, tough day in camp."

Pesach gave me a funny look. "Camp is fun. What do you do when you come from camp?"

"I take a snack, play with my computer, maybe watch some TV. Then my parents come, we have dinner, I read."

Pesach stared at me.

"But it is not raining out today. It is not cold. And no *hamsin*."

"*Hamsin*?"

"Very hot desert winds. In Israel when I was your age, I did not come home until I had to. For dinner or because of dark."

I didn't say anything, but I felt like saying, "Well, this isn't Israel, buddy, and I do things the American way."

"Come. You will take me to park."

"No."

"I do not understand. First, you are happy because your friend Ted is home, but now you do not want to go see him?"

"It's none of your business." I stomped off toward my room. I turned on my computer. I clicked on a game and heard my cousin in the hallway. I felt bad about being sort of mean to him.

"You can come in and see my computer, if you want."

He came in without a word and watched me play my game. I offered him a turn, and he didn't even ask what to do. He just took the mouse and started playing.

"Did you play this game before? In Israel or something?"

"No, I just try it after watching you." He played for a few minutes and then stood up. "I want to go to the park. I want to see this country. If you do not want to go, maybe you can make me a map. I will go myself."

I took a piece of paper and started to draw a dumb kind of map. It was getting tricky. I figured it was almost easier to show him.

"Look," I explained, "the park is not near. It is far, actually. It would take us forever to get there."

"We can take bikes. You have extra bike for me?"

I couldn't tell him the truth, that I didn't know how to ride.

"No, we don't. Uh, okay, we'll walk."

Next thing you know we were walking to the park.

Pesach was thrilled. I wasn't. I couldn't believe I was in this mess, though I did like the thought of seeing Ted.

While we walked, Pesach looked around. He was amazed at everything. What got to him most was that so many houses were made out of wood.

"We never build houses from wood. Only stone, and

in Jerusalem we have special stones, Jerusalem stone, very beautiful."

I looked at the houses, and they looked good to me, wood or no wood. I thought they were pretty terrific looking, though I hadn't really given it much thought before.

"Where are the people?"

"What people?"

"If there are houses, there must be people, no? Is everyone on holiday?"

"What?" I asked.

"Did all the people go away on holiday?"

Finally, I figured out what he meant. He expected to see people in the street, and of course, there weren't any, except a few really young kids. I explained to him that in my neighborhood, people don't really hang out in the streets. We just sort of get into our cars and go where we are going.

"So how do you get to know all your neighbors?"

"You don't."

He gave me a puzzled look that I was sort of getting used to.

We were interrupted by a shriek.

9

ANOTHER GREAT IDEA

It was Ted. He'd seen me as we approached the ball field in the park. He was pitching, but he dropped the ball, called "Time-out!" and ran over to me, jumping and slamming me on the back.

"Hey, Seym, am I glad to see you. You look great. Hey, you even have some color in your cheeks. When is your cousin coming?"

I interrupted him quickly, 'cause I'd written to him that I was less than thrilled about my cousin coming and I sort of didn't want to hurt Pesach's feelings now that he was standing right there in the flesh and blood.

"This is my cousin. Pesach, meet Ted. Ted, meet Pesach."

"Hallo, Ted." Pesach smiled. "So this is baseball? If I watch for a few minutes and learn the rules, maybe could I play for some time?"

"You mean you don't have baseball in Israel?" Ted and I asked at about the same time.

"No. Our big sport is football. No, wait, I remember you call it soccer. We call it football because you play with your foot. And basketball is next. I am very good at soccer, but I have never really seen baseball."

"Sure, ah, Pess . . . I forgot your name."

I helped Ted say Pesach about ten times till he could say it right. Then we went over and sat down to watch the game. I was hoping it would take Pesach a zillion and a half years to figure out the game so that he really wouldn't want to play, since I certainly didn't want to.

Unfortunately, Pesach seemed to be a great learner and observer. Even though I did try to complicate things a bit, after two innings he suddenly stood up and announced, "Ted, I'm ready."

Ted called time-out and put Pesach on his team. He told him he could play outfield because that was the easiest position. (That's the spot I always get.) Then Ted turned to me. "Do you want to play, Seymour?"

I actually started to say, "No, you need someone to be a fan," when Pesach chimed in.

"Of course he wants to play. He only sat before to explain rules to me."

So Pesach played and I played until I got hit in the arm with a fastball and had to retire. Pesach wasn't too terrific, either, but he sure was better than I was after many long years of trying. And every time he got up at bat, he looked better and better, until finally he actually hit a double, and though at first he forgot that he was supposed to run, he made up for a slow start with a great sprint. I decided we must be so distantly related that our genes had nothing in common anymore.

Finally, the game was over. Ted's team won, and Pesach was really enjoying it. All the kids got on their bikes to leave, and Pesach and I started walking home. I don't think I'd had so much exercise in one day since I was born.

We had just gotten past the park gate when Pesach stopped and said, "*Ben-dodi*, we don't want to walk back the way we came."

I agreed. I didn't want to walk. But since there was no car or train or taxi waiting to take us home, I was sort of puzzled.

"My folks won't be home yet to give us a ride," I explained.

"Ride? No, no. I don't want to ride, but we shall go a different way back, okay?"

"I don't know a different way back. This is the direct route."

"What do you mean 'direct'?"

"In Hebrew is there an expression that means the shortest distance between two points is a straight line?"

"Yes, of course: *yashar.* 'Direct' means it is short way to go?"

"Well, I wouldn't exactly call this a short walk, but it is

the shortest way I know. In fact, it is the only way I know."

Pesach laughed.

"This is not long, Seym. In Israel, once a year, we walk for four days, forty kilometers a day. That is more than twenty miles a day. It is called Tsa'ada. I have done this."

"Why would you do that?" I asked.

"It's a tradition in Israel," he answered.

I was glad I was born in America, but I didn't want to hurt the guy's feelings, so I ignored that remark.

"Come, we will find a new way." And with that he turned down a corner and started off down a street that was totally unfamiliar to me.

"But, Pesach. There is no point to this. Come on, let's go the way I know. My folks will get worried if we take a few days to get home."

"Seym, that was good joke, but I think you doubt, how you say, our ability to find another way."

"I don't know about your ability, but I know about mine. Direction is not one of my major talents. In fact, sometimes my mom says that if she turned me around twice in my room, she thinks I'd get lost finding the door."

Pesach didn't laugh; he just looked at me funny.

"It is only because no one taught you. In Israel you would learn this early in *tzofim*, uh, what you call 'scouts,' and then of course in the army you would have to learn to find your way by day or night in strange places. I will teach you."

He then went into this whole long thing about figuring out directions by the place of the sun in the sky and the stars and landmarks and a zillion other informative things. I tried to pay attention, but secretly I just felt a little scared walking around strange streets. I figured Pesach might know his way around Israel, but he certainly wouldn't know his way around Merrick, New York. I wasn't sure he even knew the name of my street, so how in the world would we ever get home?

I figured that eventually my parents would organize a search party and come searching for us, but by then we might have died of starvation or something. I didn't want to insult my cousin, but I was sure this was a very dumb idea, and the more I thought about it, the more I thought about how it was dumb of my parents to even invite this guy over with his strange habits and lectures.

"Wait, I see something."

I tried to follow my cousin's gaze, but I saw nothing familiar, just a teenage girl bent over her bike a few driveways down. Before I knew what was happening, we were standing in front of the driveway and my crazy cousin was talking to the girl. She seemed startled at first, but after looking at me, she seemed to decide she could talk to us, or, rather, listen to him.

"You have trouble with bicycle?"

The girl stood up and looked at us, at me and at him and then at me and then at him. Finally, she said, "Yes, I think I have a flat tire."

"I can look at it?"

"It's not necessary," she said, moving between us and the bike. "My father will take it off, and we'll bring it into the repair shop."

"Repair shop? Why?"

Before she could answer, Pesach was by the bicycle looking at the wheel, squeezing it. I was embarrassed.

"You have screwdriver?"

"No, really. It isn't necessary. My father will do it."

"No problem. My cousin and I can fix it. I am sure."

Now he'd really gone too far. Since I couldn't even ride a bike, I would be the last person in the world who could fix one.

But Pesach just went on. "You know my cousin Seymour? You are neighbors." The girl looked at me questioningly. "You know the Goldfarb family?"

The girl started to say "No," but then said, "Oh sure, Dr. Goldfarb. I didn't know we were neighbors."

"We're not, exactly. I live over on Monroe Drive," I explained.

But the girl wasn't even listening anymore. It was as if my cousin had hypnotized her. She went in the garage and came out with a whole bunch of tools. Next thing I knew Pesach had the wheel off and she was filling a bucket with water from the hose. He told her to do it, and she just did. They both seemed to have forgotten that I was there, except every once in a while, Pesach would say, "Right, Seymour?" And I would just stare at the pair of them.

Pesach took the tire off the rim and dipped it in the water. Bubbles spouted, and he proclaimed, "Now we know where it is broken. We fix it." He rummaged around the garage. "Today I just make temporary fix, tomorrow I get what I need to fix it. Seymour will show me where. You have, oh, how you say, *masheva*—to put air back?"

"Pump," the girl volunteered and then asked him where he was from. She seemed really interested that he was from Israel. But all I was interested in was getting home.

I couldn't take their jabbering, though I guess I couldn't blame my cousin. The girl was really kind of pretty, if you like long hair and a great face and stuff. But she was too old for me, and I was still worried about getting home. I was sure it would be dark soon, and then we might be lost forever. I figured I had better find the pump so we could get out of there.

I interrupted their chatter. "Did you say you had a pump?"

"Uh, I think so. I think it's in the shed in back of the house."

I was so eager to get home that I forgot to think clearly about all the 160 reasons that a person should not go exploring in another person's backyard. So I went in the back and started to open the shed door.

The sound of barking, fierce, big-dog-type barking, suddenly sounded loud and clear. My heart started beating the fastest it had ever beaten almost, not counting the great boat ride at camp. I was so scared that I couldn't tell whether the ferocious dog noises were coming from in the shed, behind the shed, or near the shed. I was frozen to the spot, with my hand on the latch of the shed door. I was too terrified to move. Then I heard a voice.

"Who are you, and just what do you think you are doing in my shed?"

I turned around and practically fainted. Standing there, right there in the teenage girl's yard, in front of the teenage girl's shed, was Lari—the beautiful, perfect Lari.

And as if that wasn't bad enough, attached to Lari's hand was the biggest, hairiest dog I had ever seen. It had so much hair that I wasn't sure it had a face under there, but it kept barking and lurching on the leash that Lari was holding. It looked as if it could eat up a kid like me in five seconds flat.

So what did I do? Well, of course I was scared, more

scared than I am even under normal conditions. I mean this was like a nightmare, except I had the awful feeling that I wasn't dreaming. I could feel the dog's breath every time he lunged at me. What should a guy do?

What other guys would do, I don't know. They would probably leap over the shed and escape or just pet the dog and say, "Cute dog you've got there," and the dog and the girl would fall instantly under the guy's spell. But not me, that's not my style. I just sneezed. Yeah, sneezed. Remember, I told you I'm, like, highly allergic. So I started sneezing like crazy and my eyes started watering and I stood there like a complete idiot. Sneezing and drooling. The dog was so shocked he stopped barking and sat down.

By then, hearing all the commotion, my untrustworthy cousin and the girl he'd hypnotized were also in the backyard. Everybody was talking at once.

"Lari, what are you doing?" (The teenage girl.)

"Oy vey." (Pesach.)

"Ahchoo." (Me.)

"Morgan was barking and I saw this kid Seymour poking around the shed, so I came out with Morgan to investigate." (Lari.)

Through my sneezes and Pesach's oy veys and the girls' chattering, I am still pretty sure that I actually heard Lari mention my name. She knew my name. For a moment, the thought made me happy. I don't know why. Then I realized that made it worse. She'd know what name to report to the police when she called to report me for trespassing or attempted snooping or something.

It took a few seconds and a lot of sneezing by me and explaining by everyone else till the whole thing was cleared up. It seems that the girl with the bicycle was Bari, who was Lari's older sister. I was going to ask if their parents' names were Shari and Harry, but I didn't think the girls would appreciate my joke, and my cousin probably wouldn't even get the point, so I said nothing.

Besides, in addition to being too busy sneezing to talk clearly, I was too embarrassed in front of Lari to say anything that would even resemble normal human speech. Bari explained to Lari that I'd just been helping Pesach, who in turn was just helping her. Lari believed her, I guess. Eventually, Bari took her eyes off my cousin long enough to notice that I was still in the midst of a ridiculous sneezing bout.

"Why, he must be allergic to dogs!" she exclaimed, sending Lari and Morgan back to the house. Pesach took his eyes off Bari for a few seconds to come over and sort of pound me on the back. That works if someone is coughing or choking, but it does nothing for sneezing, though it seemed to make Pesach and Bari feel as if I were being cared for. Lari returned with a box of tissues, which she handed to me with her arm as far away as possible while still being able to reach me. She acted like I had a contagious disease.

When I recovered and saw the two sisters standing near each other, I did notice the resemblance. They looked sort of like sisters. I thought Lari was prettier—her hair was blonder and her eyes were bluer and all—not that I really looked that hard or anything.

Bari was laughing at whatever Pesach was saying, and nobody seemed to remember anything about me, the broken bicycle, or going home. I reminded Pesach that my parents would eventually miss us, though actually from the way they'd been acting lately, I figured they'd probably only worry about my cousin.

I pictured them coming home to an empty house and saying, "Oh, where can Pesach be? No note. Maybe he went out and got lost, forgot a key. Hope his English is good enough so he won't get taken advantage of or really lost. Oh, and shouldn't that kid, what's-his-name, be home from camp soon?"

But I still wanted to get home. I was worn out, to put it mildly, and totally mortified. So I sort of grabbed my cousin and said, "Sorry, we've got to be going."

"I will come back tomorrow or next tomorrow to fix bicycle," Pesach called out to Bari as I yanked him out of the yard. Bari just smiled and nodded. I thought to myself, *Cousin, next time you come to this house, you are coming alone, alone, alone.* But I didn't say anything at all to him. I just followed his lead, hoping he really knew where he was going.

"American girls are very beautiful, right?"

I didn't answer.

He didn't seem to notice my silence and just sort of hummed a tune I'd never heard before.

10

MADRICH

I guess my cousin really knew about directions, because we did arrive home safely, though by the time we got there the aromas of a special home-cooked meal were already pouring out the front door. My father had made his famous stuffed cabbage, and my mother had made some kind of roast. It was definitely company food. That reminded me how excited they were about my cousin.

I stormed into the house and went straight to my room and kind of slammed the door. Neither of my parents came after me to see if there was anything bothering me. Guess they didn't notice because they were so preoccupied with the great Pesach. I threw out the bunch of gross tissues that I'd been carrying around with me and thought about it for a minute.

This guy really seemed to have some kind of magic about him. I'd read a book once where the main character had some kind of a special quality, a kind of charm. I tried to remember the word. I think it was *charisma*. Yeah, Pesach seemed to have this charisma. It had gotten him admiration from my parents, Ted and the guys, and that girl, Bari. I wasn't sure about Lari. I had tried to avoid looking at her as much as possible. Some guys have all the luck, I thought.

He gets the charisma and I get the phobias, and we're supposed to be related to each other!

I considered saying I felt sick when my parents called "Supper!" But since my folks are doctors, they can really tell if you're sick. Besides, I was hungry. So I allowed them to have the pleasure of my company.

Naturally, they didn't appreciate my company. They were babbling on and on with Pesach about people in Israel whom I didn't know and family in the States whom Pesach didn't know and politics in Israel and politics here and other junk.

I figured that they had forgotten all about me, like maybe I had become invisible or something. I looked down at my arm. I could see it. Maybe I wasn't invisible. Or maybe I was the only one who could see me. It sure seemed that way. If I hadn't been such a chicken about life and adventure, I think I would have considered running away. But I was too scared to think of even walking away.

Suddenly, I realized that my name was being mentioned.

"That sounds like a great idea. Seymour will love it," said my father.

"What will Seymour love?" I asked. I'd gotten so used to not paying attention to the boringness of what they were saying that I'd stopped listening completely.

"Being my *madrich*," said Pesach. "Like today."

Today didn't sound so terrific to me. I had a feeling that I'd heard that word *madrich* before, and it hadn't been good then.

"What's a *madrich*?" I had to know.

"'Tour guide.' I told you before once. Remember?"

"Yes, I do remember. I remember walking for seventeen years to and from the park and nearly getting killed by a hairy dog as big as an elephant, and getting lost and sneezing."

"I will keep you away from dogs," Pesach said, laughing.

"That shouldn't be a problem where you're going!" my mother declared. "I don't think they let dogs in museums or in the Empire State Building."

"Oh no!" I got up from the dinner table and seriously thought about really, truly running away. "You know that I don't like going to New York City. I hate New York City. Why should I go to the city? Why? Why? Why? Give me one good reason!"

My father stood up. He had this glazed look in his eyes. "Seymour J. Goldfarb, I do not believe this outburst. What kind of behavior is this? And in front of our guest!"

"David!" My mother stood up at the table too. "Seymour must be tired. Let me talk to him. Don't take it so seriously. Come, Seymour."

But the way she yanked me into my room, I could tell that my mom was no less angry than my dad. And when she closed the door and put her hands on her hips and her eyes started flashing, I knew she was angry— Angry, with a capital *A*.

"Seymour, I can't believe how rude and impolite you sound. Here is your Israeli cousin, fresh out of years of army duty, here for a brief vacation, and you decide to pick this time to be fresh to your parents. I'm mortified! This is not your normal behavior and not your normal tone, and I want it stopped. Do you hear me? Pesach is here to see this country, and while he is in our home, we are going to treat him royally. Since your father and I can't take off from work tomorrow, you will have to accompany him to the city. I should think that you would be honored to be kind of a junior guide, a translator, at your age. It shows that we all consider you something of a mature person, able to handle a challenge—not to mention that it should be fun! Well, what do you have to say for yourself?"

"How can I translate when I don't know Hebrew?" I said.

"Oh, you are exasperating this evening," said my

mother as she sank onto my bed. "I don't mean translate from English to Hebrew. I mean translate from slang or difficult English into simple English. I am sure that in a few days Pesach will be much more fluent in the language. Right now, it seems a little hard for him."

It didn't seem so hard when he was talking to Lari's sister, I thought, but it didn't seem like a good time to bring up that point. So I tried to make my mother understand the rest of the problem. I had to try. I felt desperate.

"Listen, Mom, I am just a kid. A little kid, you know. I don't know my way around the city, and I have never liked going to the city. I mean when Dad drives in, it is less awful, but the train and all the strange people and the crowds and everything, it sort of scares me."

My mother looked at me silently for a minute, and I thought she had a look of understanding on her face.

"Seymour, I know that the city is different for you. That is what makes it so exciting. People come from all over the world to visit New York City. We're lucky to live so close to Manhattan. We're close enough to commute to the city and yet live a quieter kind of life. I can understand your being afraid of going to the city alone, which I would never let you do—well, not for a few years, of course—but you are going with an adult. Pesach may be your cousin, but he is not a child, and I am sure he can handle any problems, if you just explain them to him."

"Sure, Mom, sure." And probably even make a few problems himself too. Running away was starting to look better and better. How could my own mother, the woman who gave birth to me, not even understand one word that I had said? It was no use. She was my last hope. I knew I had to go. And I knew I was dreading it. Just when camp was finally over and I thought that I had nothing left to worry about for about five minutes, I had a new set of worries that made the old ones seem tiny.

11

UGA, UGA, CHOO, CHOO

When I woke up, I knew I wasn't eager to get out of bed, but it took me a few minutes to remember why. When I did remember, I scrunched back down under the covers and tried to forget. My parents were surely gone by now, I decided, glancing at the clock. And I was sure that Pesach wouldn't be rude enough to barge into my room and wake me. I was wrong.

Okay, so he didn't barge in. He knocked, but he could have awakened me if I'd been sleeping, and that would have been rude, very rude. After all, this was my house, and I had just finished a long time at camp and needed some time off to rest and recuperate.

But I was the only one who seemed to think that I mattered anymore. It was Pesach this and Pesach that. To think that I was supposed to take him to the city was ridiculous, infuriating, and every other long word you can think of.

"*Boker tov, ben-dodi.*"

I knew that *boker tov* means "good morning." We'd learned that in Hebrew school.

"Yeah, good morning to you too," I murmured, trying to get back under the blankets.

"We have luck," said Pesach. "The weather is so nice. It will be great to visit your big city."

I sat up in bed.

"Listen, Pesach. Can't you go without me? I don't know my way around, you saw that yesterday. And besides, I hate New York City. It is full of bums and beggars and robbers, and it is dirty and gross."

"Hmm. I see. But you will have me, a soldier, to defend you. No one will hurt you if you are with me."

"What if we're attacked by a gang of hoodlums with chains?"

"I do not understand even one of those words—*gang, hoodlums, chains*."

"Did you ever see the old movie *West Side Story*?" I asked him.

"Oh, yes." Pesach stood up and started singing "Maria."

"I guess you saw it; you don't have to sing all the songs to prove it. Well, New York City can be like that."

"Come on, *ben-dodi*, I am not afraid. And you are with me so you are not afraid too. Get up. Get dressed. I have breakfast all ready."

I was curious to see what kind of breakfast Pesach had made. I was used to cereal and milk except on weekends.

So I forced myself to get up and wash up and everything. Besides, I was hungry. I'd sort of picked at dinner last night, and I'd missed dessert after arguing with my dad about the city.

Well, this breakfast was actually worth getting up for, if I say so myself. There were eggs and cheese and bread and a salad made of teeny-tiny pieces of cucumber and tomato and green pepper. Of course I didn't let on right away about how delicious I thought everything was. In fact, I started off by being sort of grouchy.

"What is that?" I pointed to the chopped-up vegetables.

"Salad," replied my cousin, calmly scrambling an egg.

"It doesn't look like salad," I insisted.

"Ah, but it is salad. In Israel we are not so in love with lettuce as you. Taste it; it is very good. But if you come to Israel I will make you a better one. Our vegetables and fruit are much better."

"Modest, aren't you?" I mumbled under my breath. Out loud I just informed him, "We don't eat salad for breakfast in America."

"You should," said Pesach, shoveling a sizable portion onto his plate. "Come on, you will like it. I know. It is nothing to be afraid of."

Something about the way he said that sort of aggravated me, so I tasted the salad and it really was good.

I asked him what he put on it. It didn't taste like my favorite dressing, creamy Italian, which is what I usually drown my salad in.

"Just lemon and oil, olive oil," said Pesach, quickly rinsing the dishes. "Come on, now. Let's get going. We must see New York today."

I started coughing suddenly. "I'm not feeling great. Can't you kind of go ahead without me? I'm too little to be much help anyway."

Pesach looked at me. "I can go by myself, but it would be more fun with a true American guide by my side. Come on, it will be fun. What could go wrong?"

"If I listed everything that could go wrong, we'd be here for a year," I cautioned.

"*Lo chashoov*, 'not important,'" said Pesach. "I am guest, and you must be good to guest. No more wasting of time."

So, despite my better judgment and my extreme worried state, I soon found myself at the train station with Pesach and two round-trip tickets to Manhattan. I hoped we'd survive the experience long enough to be able to use the second half of the round-trip. As we stood on the platform, waiting for the train to pull in, I had my doubts.

But we did get on a train, and it was a train going in the right direction, so as Pesach and I sat and looked out the window, I began to relax. That calm feeling lasted about three seconds. It ended when Pesach pulled out his phone and began scrolling through it.

"What are you doing?" I asked.

"I have a list, in Hebrew, of what to see in New York."

"Can I see it?"

Every museum you could think of was on that list, plus the United Nations, South Street Seaport, Greenwich Village, the New York Public Library, Macy's (the World's Largest Store), the Empire State Building, and the World Trade Center.

"Listen, it would take you weeks to see everything on that list. You don't want to do the whole thing in one day, do you?"

"No, no, we will take several days. Your parents say we should go to Museum of Modern Art or Museum of Natural History or Metropolitan, and Empire State."

"Fine," I breathed with a sigh of relief. "You pick one of those museums. Any one is fine with me."

"I will look them up in my book and choose." Pesach turned back to his guide. "Fine, Museum of Modern Art today and Empire, and of course Statue of Liberty."

I felt a strong feeling of panic return. "You have to get on a boat to go to the Statue of Liberty," I explained. "We don't have a boat."

"My book tells you everything, *ben-dodi*, don't worry.

We can take ferryboat. It even tells us exactly where to go."

"Oh no, oh no. Your book is wrong. Trust me. No ferry, no boat, no Statue of Liberty. Sorry."

Pesach closed his book. People across the aisle were looking at me. I guess I must have spoken a little loudly, to sort of emphasize my point.

"Do you want to explain to me what that was all about? Is there a reason we can't go to see the Statue of Liberty, most famous American woman? Well, you can tell me? *Nu*?"

I sighed and then I explained that I was never going on another boat ride as long as I live. "If I am reincarnated I still won't go on a boat, 'cause I'm sure I'd remember my last boat ride forever and ever and ever and ever, even in a future life," I added.

"Why you don't like boats?" he asked me.

So I told him. I told him everything about my all-too-recent boat ride around Manhattan. I gave him every gory detail, even stopping now and then to be sure I'd said it in simple enough English to be understood clearly, completely, and unmistakably.

Pesach listened. Then he burst out laughing. He was laughing so hard that everyone else in our part of the train was staring, and some people looked like they were almost laughing too. Pesach just kept laughing and hitting his leg and laughing. I was getting angrier and more embarrassed with every one of his ha-has. I turned to look out the window, just as the train went through the tunnel and the lights flickered.

"I am not laughing on you," Pesach said when he finally caught his breath. "But it does sound like a funny, how you say, adventure, *mamash beedoor*."

I was going to give him a lecture about what a sick sense of humor he must have. But then the train stopped, and I had to switch my mind over to getting around New York City.

"Last stop, Penn Station," said the conductor.

Ugh! I thought to myself. This was where I usually started to feel nervous and cling to the side of my parents, but this time those same parents had sent me here with this person with a terrible sense of humor. I was full of dread, pure dread.

12

NEW YORK, NEW YORK

We climbed up the steps that led from the track to the main part of the station. I had this sickening sensation that I always get the minute my feet hit New York City. There was noise and smoke and dirt and crowds right there in the train station, and we hadn't even hit the sidewalk. There were also all kinds of rough-looking characters, people walking around talking to themselves, and bag ladies. I don't know why those types scared me, but then again, what didn't scare me? I wished I was really rich, and then I'd donate tons of money to take care of all those people who were sleeping in the station. It couldn't be too comfortable. Pesach didn't seem afraid, though he did seem disturbed.

"Why nobody helps these people?" he asked.

I tried to explain to him about homeless people and shelters and the stuff that my parents had told me when I asked them the same question.

"Not fair. Not fair," he kept muttering, and I had to agree with that.

We were still inside the station when we passed one

of those video places where there are a zillion machines going at the same time. You could hear a zillion zaps and beeps all at once.

"Come, we go see these machines. It looks like fun."

"No, Pesach," I practically screamed, and grabbed his arm, but it was no use. He walked right in, and I wasn't about to get separated from him in the middle of Penn Station. So before I even knew what was happening, we were inside that place. I was sure we looked ridiculous—an obvious tourist in funny brown sandals and a small, terrified-looking kid in the middle of a room full of tough-looking teenagers and older guys who looked like advertisements for tattoo parlors. There were flashing lights and beeping sounds all around us.

Suddenly, I realized that my crazy cousin was talking to someone. I was scared.

I looked up to see what kind of tattoos the guy my cousin was talking to was wearing. But it was just the man who was selling tokens to play the games. Pesach paid him something, and the next thing I knew, he was playing one of the games. What could I do? I stood near him and watched him play. For a few seconds, I actually concentrated on the game he was playing. When his turn was over, I said, "Let's go."

"Now you, too, *ben-dodi*," Pesach said as he plunked another token into the machine.

I bet I would have gotten a higher score if I hadn't been so worried about my surroundings. I was glad when Pesach finally said, "Enough. We go now. See everything."

I led Pesach to the street and was about to suggest that we take a taxi, but he was busy going "Oooo" and "Ahhhh" about the tall buildings right across the street from the station.

"You know, it really looks like in the movies, just the same. I can't believe I'm here."

"I can't believe I'm here, either," I exclaimed. "I'd rather watch this stuff in the movies."

"Okay. Now we go to the Empire State Building," he said.

"I'll get us a cab," I volunteered.

Pesach gave me a look that said he didn't seem to understand.

"Taxi. I'll get us a taxi," I explained slowly, carefully pronouncing each syllable.

"We don't need a car, a taxi," said Pesach. "I looked on the Web last night, so I know we are very near Empire Building. We will walk. Let me see, Fifth Avenue must be that way. Come on, *ben-dodi*."

"If you know where you are going," I answered, huffing and puffing as I ran after him, "then why did you need me?"

"It is more fun to see things with someone else, to share, no?" he asked. "And you are my *madrich*, my guide, when I don't understand."

"Some guide," I muttered as I hurried to keep up with him. "A guide leads. I follow," I added, but he didn't seem to be paying attention. He was looking around intently, studying the people, the stores, the cars, the signs, and the traffic. At least that is what I think he was doing. I tried to imagine what he found so fascinating. To me, it was all just scary—all those people rushing about, so many different kinds of people, different shapes, sizes, colors, and all kinds of weird dress. We even passed a man who was dressed up as a hot dog. He was standing in front of a restaurant, handing out flyers about lunch. I felt sorry for the poor guy; it was hot to be dressed up with mustard and a bun.

"This is something, a talking *nak-neekiya*," Pesach said, and laughed. "How do you say *nak-neekiya*?" he asked, pointing to the guy with the flyers. So I gave him a short course in the many names for hot dog: frankfurter, frank, hot dog, and wiener. I was starting to think he might actually need my services as a translator when he suddenly proclaimed, "We're here."

Sure enough, there was the plaque, EMPIRE STATE BUILDING. We walked inside. I read the signs and explained to Pesach that we needed tickets to go all the way up, and the tickets cost money. I also showed him that there were an awful lot of people ahead of us in line.

"Maybe we should skip this place," I suggested. "Look at the lines. And why should we spend good money for tickets to go to the top of a building?" It wasn't that I was afraid of heights, well, not terribly, but high up was not one of my first choices of where to be. And I certainly didn't believe in waiting in line for such a non-fun activity.

Pesach didn't answer me, at least not right away. Instead, he asked some people who were exiting the building if they had enjoyed the view. Then he asked the ticket lady how long the line took to get to the top.

"About half an hour, but don't hold me to it," she said.

"We'll take two tickets," Pesach said, reaching for his wallet.

No one ever listens to me. So soon we were entering an elevator and then waiting in a line and then repeating the procedure. It was a lot more than half an hour till we got to the top. It was hot in all those lines, and I was far from enthusiastic when we finally made it—the eighty-sixth floor. Ugh!

"Look, *ben-dodi*," called Pesach as he made his way to the edge to capture the view. "It is grand!"

I could think of a lot of ways to describe it, but "grand" wasn't one of them.

"You know, when you parachute, it is the same type of thing. You look out, and you are so high up. Everything below is tiny, practically unrecognizable. And then you float down—what a feeling! You must try it."

I was starting to feel nauseous. All I could think of was the way it feels when you have a dream that you're falling. Your whole body feels sick, sickening, and gross. I couldn't believe that this person who was related to me actually enjoyed falling, and from great heights yet—jumping out of a plane.

I was stammering when I finally spoke. "You've really done it . . . parachuted?" I asked.

"Of course, in the army. I was lucky; not everyone gets to do it."

"We sure have different definitions of *lucky*," I mumbled.

By the time we got back down to earth, ground floor, and the outside world again, I was exhausted and ready to go home.

"Well, now that you've seen the city, we can go home," I volunteered. "It's good that we're so close to Penn Station." I pulled out a schedule and started checking the trains. "If we hurry, we can make the—"

"You are funny, my cousin," laughed Pesach. "I like that joke. If you have seen the city from the top of the Empire State Building, then you have really seen the city.

Very good joke. We go now to see art. Art we must see up close, not far. Come on."

I tried to tell Pesach that I wasn't joking; I was just hungry and tired. But he was too preoccupied with the buildings and the people. Finally, I shouted, "I'm hungry!"

"No problem," he answered, and soon I was having lunch—a hot pretzel and a can of soda bought from a stand. I hate pretzels, but the soda was okay, even though I'd meant a real lunch.

"Can't we sit down?" I asked.

"Why not?" answered my agreeable relative, dragging me over to sit on the steps of what turned out to be the New York Public Library. Even though there were plenty of people sitting there, there was enough room for us too. My mom had taken me inside that library once. There were more books in that place than probably all of our Long Island libraries together. It was awesome, but Pesach didn't want to go in there, and I was beginning to see that we would go where he wanted to go.

"Next stop, Museum of Modern Art," said Pesach, imitating the tone of the Long Island Railroad conductor. "Come on, Seymour, it's not too far."

It wasn't a long walk, if you're used to really long walks in scorchingly hot weather. By the time we got there, I would have been thrilled to go in anywhere, as long as it was air-conditioned. Pesach didn't seem to care about the air-conditioning; he was just eager to see the art. The pictures weren't too bad, though I could have done just as well myself on some of them, and I really don't know why everyone is so impressed with this guy Picasso and his chopped-up-type pictures. Pesach explained some stuff to me about styles and similarities between pictures. But between my being tired and his nonperfect English and sometimes difficult accent, I didn't get everything he tried to show me.

He didn't get what I tried to show him, either—the gift shop. There were some great-looking things in there, even watches and all kinds of stuff, but he wasn't interested. If there's one thing I believe in, it's souvenirs. I mean even if you go somewhere you hate, you should buy something to remember it by, if only to remember not to go there ever again. But grown-ups never seem to grasp that; all they see is how much it costs to get a "silly little souvenir." What I really wanted in this place was a kaleidoscope. There were some amazing ones, but I didn't have enough money with me and I didn't want to ask my cousin.

"How about lunch?" I suggested.

"You hungry already?" Pesach asked.

I was starting to wonder if I'd caught Kevin the Blob's preoccupation with food when I noticed on the clock that it was definitely, legitimately long past lunchtime.

"Aren't you hungry?" I couldn't believe I was the only one starving.

"A little. So where will you take me for lunch?"

"Me? Take you? Did you forget that I am a kid?"

Pesach laughed. "Okay, kid, find us a New York special pizza. I hear a lot about your pizza."

Now it was my turn to laugh. "Why don't you just ask somebody who works in the museum for directions to a good pizza parlor?" I offered.

"Your English is better. You are supposed to help, *madrich*, remember?"

Following the instructions of the museum lady, we finally ended up in front of food. Pesach made me order. I couldn't decide if he really was embarrassed about his English or if he was trying to get me to do something.

For someone who hadn't been hungry a little while ago, my cousin did a great job on several slices with assorted toppings, and then he even made me get him some garlic knots. Maybe he thought "a little hungry" was what we mean when we say we're starving.

After lunch, Pesach started asking me a zillion questions about all the signs we could see through the windows and what they meant. He had trouble with the word *mutual* that was in a big mutual funds sign. I knew mutual funds had something to do with money, but he wanted to know the meaning of each word by itself. It was hard explaining mutual, even though I remembered a crazy song my mother used to sing about belonging to a mutual admiration society, "my baby and me, oh." Pesach liked the song and started singing it as we marched out of the pizza place.

"Okay, time to go to Penn Station," I said. Pesach gave me a funny look.

"Why go to Penn Station, *ben-dodi*? We have so much to see and do. How about United Nations? I want to see what there is in that place that stops people from thinking clearly."

"The United Nations? I've never been there, and I'm sure there is nothing to see. If we go there, it may be dark by the time we finish."

"So there are no streetlights in New York City?"

"Yes, of course there are lights, but don't you want to call it a day?"

"Call what day? I don't understand," Pesach said. "Look, we must see one more thing. I let you decide, Statue of Liberty or United Nations."

I think he cheated on that one. Obviously, a person with my recent horrendous experience on a boat would almost rather be caught dead than on a boat to the Statue of Liberty. So that's how I found my poor tired feet dragging themselves to the United Nations.

"It's just a few blocks," my cousin kept saying.

But those few blocks were each gigantic streets that seemed to go on and on forever. I imagined arriving at the United Nations all sweaty and tired, with the soles worn off the bottom of my shoes.

At last we were there. There were all kinds of people, in all kinds of unusual dress. That part was interesting. But when we got inside and Pesach found out that there was a tour in Hebrew, I forgot how interesting the people looked. How could I go on a tour of the United Nations in Hebrew? I was probably too young to fully appreciate a tour in English. But since he was the one who wanted to see the UN in the first place, I figured the polite thing to do was to suffer in silence. But luck was on my side. The next tour in Hebrew was in two hours, and even he didn't want to wait that long.

So we joined an English tour, which, I have to admit, was sometimes actually interesting. The guide told us about how all the countries contributed works of art and stuff. But some of the information was boring, or I didn't get it. So I wasn't too upset when we left the tour after suddenly someone shouted, "Pesach Raviv, *ma ata oseh po*? What are you doing here?"

Pesach turned around, and there were two girls and a

guy, laughing and clapping my cousin on the back. They were all babbling away in Hebrew, so of course I understood nothing, even though he did stop to introduce me—"My American cousin and guide," I think he said. To me, he said, "These are my sister's friends," to which they all seemed to object strongly and laughingly. "Oh, my friends too," he added.

I thought it was pretty amazing that here we were in New York City, much closer to Long Island, my home, than Israel, Pesach's home, and yet he was the one who bumped into friends!

After they left, I asked Pesach if he wasn't similarly amazed at having found old friends by accident, halfway around the world. He laughed. "The world is a very little place," he said.

"It doesn't look so little to me," I told him.

"When you are young and small, the world can still seem big," Pesach agreed.

"Boy, you sound like a wise old man," I said.

"'Wise,' I'll take, but 'old,' never," he said as he started jabbing at me with a boxer's kind of jabs.

People were starting to look at us. Everyone else in the UN was behaving normally and talking quietly.

Pesach babbled something to his friends in Hebrew while I sat and worried about exactly what in the world he was telling them. I imagined that he was making plans for them to join us on an endless all-day, all-night trip around my least favorite city. But they all said "shalom" and left, and we were alone again.

"Well, now where?" I asked.

"Hmm, let's think." Pesach sat down on a bench in the lobby of the UN.

I decided to think fast.

"My parents are probably expecting us for dinner."

"I told them we might be late," he murmured.

"The bicycle. You promised to fix that girl's bicycle. You know, the one with the long blond hair."

Pesach looked up. "Okay. We go home. At least I should call her about fixing her bicycle, no?"

"Yes, yes, yes!" I thought I'd scream for joy. "But my feet are getting blisters on top of their blisters," I hinted.

"Maybe we take underground train, how you say, subway," he suggested.

"No subway," I almost screamed. "I'd rather walk with bleeding feet than ride a subway."

Pesach looked at me hard. "We don't need bleeding feet."

Me and my big mouth. He wouldn't take no for an answer.

"This is great opportunity for me to see a real subway. The only underground train in Israel is not underground. It's a little tramway, in Haifa, and even that I have ridden only few times. Yes, we must try subway and it will save time for getting home for dinner. You are right, *ben-dodi*."

"If I am right, we don't want the subway," I begged. But I'd noticed something about my cousin: he heard only what he wanted to hear and when he wanted to hear it. "Selective hearing," I think it's called. I had a teacher who used that expression whenever anyone said, "But I didn't hear you say we had homework!"

I wished I were back in school or even back in camp. Anything would be better than the subway. I had been on the subway once about a year ago with my father, and it had been gross, major gross.

But Pesach seemed to be impossible to persuade. He asked one of the UN security guards for directions to a subway that would take us to Penn Station.

"There is no subway right here," the guard said.

"Wonderful," I butted in. But both Pesach and the guard ignored me. The guard started pointing toward the door.

"You were right. It is wonderful," Pesach said as we walked back out into the broiling heat. "Because now we get to see something extra that we did not plan for, a bonus."

That's how I found out that we were on our way to Grand Central Station, where we could get the subway.

"You have been there?" Pesach was his usual enthusiastic self.

"No." I was my usual terrified self. "Penn Station is enough for me."

"Grand Central Station is famous," Pesach continued. "See here in my guidebook. Special architecture, arches, tunnels, big clock, used for many movie scenes."

"You've read all about it," I said. "So what's the point of seeing it? You know they say the book is often better than the movie."

"I don't get what you say. But come, you will enjoy."

I was too tense to enjoy. And it was a long, long walk.

"How much farther is this place?" I asked, as we crossed Third Avenue.

But instead of answering, Pesach pulled me into a sporting goods store. He had me explain that we wanted rubber and glue to fix a bicycle. We had to buy some kind of kit. "Do-It-Yourself Repair," it said.

"'Do it yourself,' I like that expression," my cousin said, and he kept repeating it over and over until we finally reached Grand Central Station.

Pesach was so busy admiring the high ceilings that I was hoping he'd forgotten why we were there. No such luck.

"How we get to Penn Station by subway?" he asked

the man in the information booth. My sense of doom increased as the man answered.

"Take the shuttle and then the One, Two, or Three train downtown, Seventh Avenue Line," the man said brusquely. "That will take you right into Penn Station." I was so sure that we'd end up in never-never land that I made him repeat the directions while I wrote them down.

"It's just one stop on the shuttle. And one stop on the One, Two, or Three." The man seemed impatient.

"Uh, what's the shuttle?" I asked as someone behind me said, "Hurry up, kid. You're not the only one in line."

"It's a subway train that runs back and forth between Grand Central and Times Square."

Great. Not only did we have to take a subway, we had to change and take two different subways. Our chances of getting lost were increasing.

"The shuttle is over there," the information man said, pointing.

Pesach and I descended the steps. He bought a metro card. I made sure we were in the right place.

"Is this the way to the shuttle, the one that takes you to Penn Station?" I asked the woman who sold tickets. She nodded.

We passed our tickets through the turnstiles. I looked around me. Ugh! It was major gross, or maybe worse than that. As we stood on the platform, I kept thinking about all the horror stories I'd heard on the news: "woman pushed off subway platform; man robbed in subway holdup; subway gang attacks unsuspecting quiet-type."

This is a dumb idea, I said to myself, but I said it slowly, quietly, silently. No use worrying Pesach. He didn't seem to know how to worry or to understand the basic truth that New York City is Dangerous, with a capital D. And to think, a short while ago, I'd called him "wise." It proves that you live and learn. Right now, I just wanted to live.

The subway train finally pulled up after what felt like seventy thousand years. Next thing you know we were on the train itself. It was crowded. I was terrified of losing Pesach, getting stuck in the subway doors as they closed, or having one of those awful headlines happen right there in my subway car. There were so many people in there, it was hot and everyone was sweaty, and the whole thing was awful, awful, awful. Everyone else was sweating from the heat, and I was sweating from fear! The subway finally lurched to a stop, and the whole train emptied, so we got off too.

I asked someone for directions to the One-Two-Three Seventh Avenue Line and kept repeating the question with every three steps we took, to be sure we were going the right way. An elderly man asked where we were going and explained that we needed the downtown track. "Then take either the Number One train, the Number Two train, or the Number Three train. They all go to Penn Station."

Thankfully, because of that man's help and my persistent checking, we ended up on the right platform. We jammed into the Number Two train when it came, and one stop later, we were jostled out to the welcoming sign:

PENN STATION 34TH STREET

Pesach and I followed the signs to the Long Island Railroad. I started breathing normally again. My cousin was totally oblivious to the danger we had just survived.

"See, *ben-dodi*, the subway is nothing to be scared from, right?" he asked.

"Well, actually," I started to explain, but by then we were rushing to catch the train to Merrick. It was already on the track. I checked and rechecked ten times that we were on the right track and on the right train. My feet were begging me to sit down. But there were no available seats on the train. We had to stand all the way home! Ugh! What a day!

Pesach wanted to walk home from the station, but I told him my parents would be upset if we didn't call, so we called. My dad picked us up.

It was so wonderful to be home, safe, and eating

dinner that I didn't have any energy to go into the agonies I'd just suffered, all because of my parents' and Pesach's dumb idea about my going into the city. I just ate and ate, but I did manage to say, "No city tomorrow, right?"

"Right!" They all laughed.

I went to sleep looking forward to a wonderful, peaceful day at home.

13

TRAPPED

I should have realized that any day with Pesach around couldn't be peaceful.

"We will go fix Bari's bicycle," Pesach announced at breakfast.

"I don't think so," I muttered. "My legs are worn out from yesterday. I can't walk that far. You go ahead without me."

"No problem," said Pesach. "I know you don't like to walk. We can take bicycles."

I started choking on my food. How could a person who voluntarily jumps out of a plane with only a parachute understand a person who is terrified of falling off a bicycle? He'd never understand, never.

"No, we don't have enough good bikes, and besides, riding a bike would hurt my legs too, and I need a day of rest . . ." I was sort of chattering away.

"I saw two bikes in the garage." He looked at me in a funny way. "One looks right size for you."

One was my size. My father got it for me before he gave up trying to teach me to ride, but, unfortunately, he never got rid of it.

I was in big trouble. If I said the bike needed air in its tires, good old resourceful Cousin Pesach would fill it up with air. If I said it had a flat tire, he could certainly see that it didn't, and even if I sneaked out and punctured the tire, he had a repair kit ready and waiting. I was trapped and I panicked.

"Listen, it's just that I sort of promised that I would spend some time with Ted today. You know, my friend you met at the park."

"Good. So you and Ted come along, and then we can all do something together."

Boy, this guy was hard to convince.

"Uh, no, I might go somewhere with Ted and his mother. Yes, I am going with Ted and his mother. Besides, remember I'm allergic to Bari's dog."

Pesach looked as if he was going to say something, but then he walked over to the kitchen sink, washed a dish, and finally said, "So, yes, I'll go to Bari's without you. You go play with Ted. A boy should go with friends his own age."

I was starting to feel guilty, that maybe I had hurt his feelings, but there was no way out of it. I told myself he'd have a fine time with Bari, and I would have a fine time alone at home, reading, playing with my computer, maybe a little TV.

And that's sort of what happened. I mean, I did do all those things alone. Ted did call, but he called to invite me to the beach, and swimming in the ocean is definitely something I try to avoid. I told him I needed to be a host for my cousin. He suggested taking my cousin along, but I told him he was out and I had to wait for him. So Ted didn't argue, and the day went quietly, peacefully, maybe a little boring, but nothing frightening.

Pesach came in about half an hour before my parents usually get home.

"Hi!" I called out. "That must have been a difficult tire to fix. It took you all day."

He gave me a weird look. "Why you don't tell me the truth? You just didn't want to be with me!"

"What do you mean?" I asked. "When? What are you talking about?"

"You said you go with Ted. But I saw Ted. He was at the beach."

"You went to the beach?" I gasped.

"After I fixed Bari's bike, we rode to the beach. I saw Ted. He said hello and asked me where you were. I said hello and said I thought you were with him."

Uh-oh. I'd gotten myself wrapped up in a few too many excuses.

"Well, Ted did call and I was going to go to the beach, but I thought maybe you'd be back early."

"*Ben-dodi*, something here is not kosher in this story. Maybe you just do not want to be with me. I can understand that. It does not have to be. I will not bother you too much more. Tomorrow your parents are making family party. The next day I go with a friend to see some things in US."

"No, no, Pesach. You don't understand. It has nothing to do with you." I started speaking before I knew what I was saying. "I do like you. Please don't leave because of me. You can stay here. I will even go to the city with you."

Pesach looked at me for a few seconds before he spoke.

"You want to go to the city with me? I thought you didn't like city. You didn't look like you like it. You looked like you don't like most anything there."

"It's not exactly that I didn't like it. I guess it was sort of fun in the end. It's just that the city scares me." I walked into the kitchen and poured a glass of juice. "You want some?" I hollered.

Pesach came in and sat down at the kitchen table. "Maybe I start to understand," he said. "It's not that you don't like it; you were afraid of it." Suddenly he jumped up, grabbed me by the shoulders, and spun me around. "Bicycles, too, right?"

"Right," I sort of whispered and didn't dare look up to see his face. Instead, I stared at his feet in those weird leather sandals.

"You are *pachdan*. No problem."

"What's *pachdan*?" I asked, though I was worried about the answer.

"Somebody who is afraid of everything. I mean afraid of many things. How do you say it in English?"

"Chicken," I said softly.

"What?"

"Chicken. I am a chicken." I screamed out the word as tears started stinging my eyes. And in two seconds I'll be a crybaby, too, I thought to myself.

"Like the kind you eat? Like barbecue?"

I'd almost forgotten that my cousin was as much interested in learning the English language as he was in learning about me, or maybe more.

"Why it is the same word?" he continued.

"How should I know?" I yelled. "I don't know everything. In fact, I don't know anything." I made a quick dash for the hallway, my room, my bed, and tears.

"Not so fast." He was right behind me in a few giant steps, and his hand was on my shoulder.

"We are cousins, yes?"

"Yes, but so what?"

"So you and I have same blood and DNA or what-you-call-it."

"Genes. The same genes."

"Like Levi's 501?"

"No, same sound, different word. Genes." I spelled it for him and explained about homonyms.

"You are good English teacher, *ben-dodi*."

"What good is a chicken even if it can teach English?"

We both laughed. "We are same genes, so you can be just like me. No *pachdan*. No chicken. I can make you strong. If you were in Israel, you would go to *tzofim*, 'scouts.' You would be more outside. You would go to army. They would make strong guy out of you."

"I don't think the whole Israeli army could make a strong guy out of me. I would flunk the test for admission to the army."

"No test. You breathe, you go. I can help you. I can help you get over chicken problem. What do you think?"

"I think you're nuts."

"What does it mean? Nuts we eat. Everything in English is food. What does nuts mean? Opposite of chicken?"

I burst out laughing. "Nuts is crazy, cuckoo, insane, weird, off-the-wall."

"Okay. You must teach me all those new words. I know crazy, but off-the-wall, that is new too. You teach me what I need to know, and I teach you what you need to know. Okay?"

"I don't see how you can teach me to not be a chicken. I'm even afraid of the idea."

"This is worse than I thought," Pesach said, laughing.

"You are afraid not to be afraid. This is very funny, no?"

"I guess it does sound funny," I admitted. "Okay. You make a plan, and if it is not too terrible, I guess I'll try. I can't get worse. I don't think anything will help, but who knows? You come from the land of miracles, right? If Moses could part the sea, maybe Pesach can do something too."

"Right," he said. "We start tomorrow morning." Then he mumbled something to himself in Hebrew. Probably wondering what he'd gotten himself into.

My parents walked in then, so I didn't ask Pesach what he'd said to himself. In fact, neither of us mentioned this new plan at all that night. I was glad that Pesach had realized I wouldn't want to discuss my problem in front of my mom and dad. Besides, they were all busy planning for the big family party the next day. It looked as if we'd be so involved with getting the house ready and preparing food that Pesach might even forget about his goal to make me more of a *gever* and less of a chicken.

I went to sleep that night worrying about what his plan would be and worrying that he might not forget about it. But somewhere deep inside me there was a little gleam of hope that he wouldn't forget, that he would wave a magic wand, and that I would be transformed into a mini Pesach: strong, brave, and even eager to parachute. If only it could happen.

14

FALLING

If dreams mean anything, I guess I was more worried than excited. I dreamt that we were in a plane and Pesach was teaching me the art of being brave. We were sitting by the door of the airplane, which was partially open. I was wearing a bunch of stuff, which I guess was a parachute.

"Now when I count to five, you will jump," he said.

"Could you make that five hundred?" I suggested. "I'm not quite ready."

"Sure you are," my dream cousin assured me. "One, two, three, four, five."

I didn't jump. I just started to shake. "I can't, I can't. I've got to get out of here," I told him.

"You can do it. You will do it. After you do it, you will feel wonderful about yourself."

"I won't live long enough to feel wonderful about myself. I'll have a bum parachute. It won't open. I won't float. I'll crash." I tried to move back into the interior of the plane.

But my cousin blocked me. "I won't let you give up. Your parachute is fine. I checked it myself. We try again.

You are ready. You will fly. You will love it. Now, one, two, three, four, five."

I didn't jump, but he pushed me. I was out of the plane, falling, falling. I wasn't sure I remembered when and how to pull the parachute cord. I tried not to panic. I tried to remember what to do. But I was so absorbed by that awful falling feeling . . .

I woke up with a start. I was sweating. The feeling of falling had been so strong that it was a relief to realize I was actually alive, in my own home, and in my own bed.

I glanced at the clock in my room. It was 3:28. That meant I had a whole night left to fly, to fall. Ugh! I didn't want to continue this nightmare, though I was curious to know if I would have survived. I wasn't curious enough, though, to want to get back into the dream. I just wanted to fall back into a dreamless sleep, so I'd have enough energy to deal with my real cousin and his real plans. He couldn't get me in a plane, no way. That couldn't be part of his real plan. Or could it? I lay there and worried awhile, and I guess I eventually drifted off back to sleep, though when I finally woke up, I didn't feel rested at all.

"What's wrong with you? Are you sick?" my mother asked when I finally emerged from my room. She was dusting, vacuuming, and straightening up in an acute frenzy. When she gets like that, my dad says she is in her "company mood," but actually, he is no better. From the kitchen I could hear the sounds of pots, pans, water, food processing, and refrigerator-opening all at once. You'd think they were preparing for a visit from the royal family, instead of just my plain old family.

"Why do you think I'm sick?" I asked my mother loudly, trying to be heard over her nonstop vacuuming.

"You slept through all this noise and, well, you don't look so terrific."

"I don't feel so terrific, either," I started to say.

"You look good to me," Pesach said, appearing suddenly out of nowhere. "And when you've eaten breakfast, you'll look even better. You are fine, fine, fine."

I thought of telling him about my dream. Would he laugh? Maybe he'd just think it was a great idea. Then he'd call Israel and arrange for a friend to bring over a plane with an extra parachute. I decided I had better not mention the dream.

"I'm not really hungry," I said softly.

"Come on. A good breakfast starts a good day. And makes a good body."

Uh-oh. That sounded like something a gym teacher might say. My cousin must have really remembered his plan to fix me.

I ate breakfast amid all kinds of carrying-on in the kitchen. My father was marinating chicken and cubing beef for another marinade.

"Where are my shish kebab sticks?" he shouted to my mother the vacuumer. If she kept vacuuming like that, there would soon be no threads left in the carpet.

Usually my parents find a thousand things for me to do when they are making a feast. It's always "Seymour, could you run and get me . . ." or "Seymour, take this upstairs, downstairs, etc." And "Seymour, fold the napkins, set the table, find the pickle dish." I'd forgotten how crazy they get. I wasn't even finished with breakfast yet when they started in with their demands.

"Seymour, ask your mother where she put the turmeric," my father said.

"What's turmeric?"

"A spice. Never mind, just ask your mom quick. I need to put it in the marinade, and the marinade has to sit for a while."

"But why can't you ask her, Dad? I'm eating."

My father rinsed his hands in the sink and turned around to stare at me. "Your mother can't hear with all her vacuuming, and I have too much to do to leave the kitchen. You should have been up earlier and eaten breakfast with us. No back talk, Seymour. Just do what I ask you and do it now."

I went to my mother and asked her about that dumb spice and then found it for my father.

"Can I help too?" asked Pesach.

"You are a guest. You didn't come to America just to help us."

"But this party is because I am here. I want to help."

"No, no, go out and have some fun."

"Can I take Seymour with me, then?" Pesach asked.

I made a silent prayer for my father to say, "No, we need him."

My father thought about it for a while. "Sure, why not?"

Traitor! My own father was pushing me out the door, into danger.

"But, Dad, you need me," I reminded him.

"I guess I can spare you for a couple of hours," my father said. "But I would like both of you back no later than that."

I started to protest. For the first time in my life, I wanted to be there, helping them. It would be bad, but I was convinced that whatever my cousin had in mind would be worse.

But my father insisted that I go out with Pesach to keep him company. "He's our guest. Be good to him."

"I'm your child; be good to me," I wanted to shout. But it was no use. I had to go with my cousin. Go to learn how not to be so afraid of everything. And here I was too afraid to even learn how to be unafraid. What a mess!

"Don't worry, Seymour and I will be back in two hours," Pesach assured my father as he all but dragged me out of the house.

"Uh, wait a minute. I need a sun hat."

"You don't need nothing!" Pesach said.

"You don't need anything!" I corrected him.

"Right! We both don't!" He smiled.

"The bathroom. I forgot to go to the bathroom," I insisted.

"A *gever*, a guy, doesn't worry about things like that," my cousin answered. "We'll find a clump of trees. You go there and do your thing."

"That is gross! Gross! Gross! Gross!"

"What this means, this gross?"

"Disgusting, revolting, awful, icky," I explained.

"I like that." Pesach laughed. "Some fun new words. See, I help you and you help me."

"Urinating on a tree is your idea of helping me?" I asked. "Some help. The only thing that would help is it would help kill a tree."

"Good joke, *ben-dodi*. But we are wasting time. We must get going. Come on."

"Where are we going?"

"You have to help me decide. We can go to park, or we can start right here with the bicycle."

"You mean you would teach me how to ride a bicycle

here in the street?" Even my cousin couldn't have that dumb an idea.

"I can't teach you in the house. So what do you think?"

"I think that this whole thing is a mistake and that I should go home and help my parents get ready for the party they are working on for you."

My cousin grabbed me by the shoulder. "No. We make deal. You will be *gever*. Stop fighting and try. Maybe you will like it."

"I don't want to make a fool of myself trying to learn to ride a bike in front of everyone. No one knows I don't know how to ride!" I blurted out angrily.

"How can they not know?" Pesach asked.

"I make up great excuses," I explained. "Everyone believes me. No one knows that I am a *pachdan* chicken."

"Hmm." My cousin looked serious. "Maybe you are very good at excuses. This maybe can be. But maybe your friends just don't tell you what they know. Maybe they don't want you to know what they know about you."

I sat down on the front steps. I felt as if I'd just been hit in the stomach. I'd never thought of that possibility. I had done a great cover-up job. How could anyone know that I was a chicken? Pesach must be wrong. He was just saying that to inspire me. It had to be.

I'd never discussed this with anyone before—not even with Ted or my parents. So that meant that even they hadn't noticed. But what if they had? Maybe Pesach was right, and they all suspected. Maybe. That was as scary a thought as being scared. If he was right, then I really did need help, and fast.

But at the same time, there was no way I was going to have bike riding and bravery lessons right there in my own neighborhood for everyone to see and laugh at.

"Even if you are right and my friends do suspect that I'm a little . . . timid, that's one more reason not to do dumb things right here in the middle of my neighborhood. I can't let everyone see what a baby I really am!"

"I have plan. No one will see," Pesach said as he dashed back into the house. "I come right back."

I don't know what he said to my father, but he must have said something. Pesach returned with the keys to my father's car and directions on his phone.

"Come on, get in. We have too little time."

I followed as if hypnotized. My father never lets anyone drive his car. It's his pride and joy. It's a stick shift, so even my mother won't drive it.

"But how'd you get the car? And where are we going? Do you have a license to drive in America?" I remembered to ask as we pulled out of the driveway. But by then it was too late.

15
PESACH'S PLAN

Pesach had no trouble with my father's car. He zoomed around like he was a race car driver who'd been driving that thing for years. He even opened the sunroof and started singing. I kept rechecking my seat belt and praying. And to think I used to be afraid of boats. If I'd known this was going to happen, I might have agreed to try Pesach's plan in my own neighborhood.

"Slow down. We have speed limits here," I called out. "Red light means stop!" I shouted. "Don't they have red lights in Israel?"

"Of course." Pesach laughed. "I am good driver. People here a little too cautious. That can be dangerous, you know," he explained as we passed a perfectly normal, healthy car and driver. "Too slow you can get killed."

"That's not what I've heard," I murmured, closing my eyes.

"Okay, we're here." Pesach zoomed past a sign that said something about County Park.

"How in the world did you find this place? And where are we?"

"Your father told me name of park and where it is on the map. Read a map and you can go anywhere, do anything."

"Gee, that might be more useful than learning not to be scared. So how about a map-reading lesson now?" I suggested.

"No more wasting time with these funny ideas. Come on."

"But you didn't even bring a bicycle. So what are you going to teach me?"

"We start little bit, easy. Build up muscles, ability, you know. Then you can just get on and ride."

I was beginning to have my doubts that this plan would work. My cousin seemed to be very confident that one, two, three and I'd be cured. If only he was right— but I knew better. I was scared deep in my bones and had been scared since the day I was born, probably, or maybe before that. Yeah, my mom says I was born more than a week later than my due date. I was probably even afraid to be born. How could anyone cure that problem one, two, three?

But I wanted to be cured and I was willing to try, sort of, as long as nothing frightening was involved. So I followed Pesach to a big field. I was out of breath by the time we got there.

"Now we start by running. Run to that tree and back."

I looked in the direction he was pointing, but it looked awfully far away. "Don't you think that's a bit far to start off with?"

"Stop talking and move. Run, now, there," he barked at me.

I started running. This must be what it's like to be in the army, I thought. Someone yells, "Move," and you get going. I was glad that I wasn't in a country where you have to get drafted. I didn't think I could handle that.

I was panting long before I got to the tree. It was so far away I kept thinking Pesach must have had a trick for moving it while I was trying to get near it! When I got there, I sort of collapsed against the rough bark. I heard a noise and realized it was Pesach again. He was signaling me. I finally realized he was telling me to come back, so I started out toward him, though I was dripping with perspiration.

But he still kept making noises and signaling. Then I realized that he actually expected me to run again, all the way back. Give a kid a break, I thought. But he kept waving his arms and stuff, so I sort of tried to run back. He didn't realize that I was running.

"Why did you walk back? I signal you to run," said my cousin the director.

"That was running," I explained as I collapsed on the ground. "Water, water, water."

"Hmm, we must go get you water. Over there, I think is fountain."

"Please bring me water. I can't move. I couldn't crawl another inch."

"What is crawl?"

"Like a baby moves," I explained, gasping for air.

"You not baby!" he yelled. "No baby. No crawl. No sit. You just need practice and slow down. Come. We run together this time."

I didn't think I could even stand up. I was starting to hate Pesach again. Who invited him, anyway?

"I will make you *gever*, if you like it or not." He pulled me to my feet. "There can be no *pachdanim*, chickens, in my family, even in American side of family."

"Remind me, what's a *gever*?"

"A man. No more talk. Come on. We run."

"You run. I'll watch. I'll learn how to do it by watching."

"You crazy, lazy kid. All Americans this bad?"

"Watch what you say!" I screamed. "Don't say anything to make me angry, or you'll be sorry."

"Good! You are alive enough to be angry. Okay. I give you little break from running. We try something easy, good for making you into *gever*, and you can rest while you do it." There was a twinkle in his eye that should have made me suspicious, but "rest" was such a tempting idea. He continued. "I stand behind you, and you fall into my arms. I will catch you."

It sounded simple enough, and I was too tired to think of my usual million reasons why it might be dangerous. So I agreed to try it.

But it was far from simple. What he meant was that I was supposed to fall backward into his arms, without bending my legs or breaking the fall in any other way.

"Trust me," Pesach kept repeating. "Just relax." I kept trying to, but I don't think relaxing is something I've ever known how to do. And mixing relaxing with falling is certainly something I'd never done.

"This is dumb. I don't see what this has to do with making me a *gever* man," I insisted after about the fiftieth time I'd tried to fall and failed. "It's just some dumb game."

"If you are so smart, you would ride bike now like regular kid your age. It is dumb to be afraid! We will fix you if you like it or not. This may not be best way, but it is my way, and we will try it. You promised. You have better idea?"

I sat down. I was tired and angry. "Yeah, I have a better idea. I will just change my name. Seymour is a stupid, wimpy name. If I change it to Stuart or Stanley, I'll be fine. That's all I need to do. Yes, I'll just change my name."

Pesach smiled and sat down beside me. He started fiddling with a twig. "I don't know what *wimpy* means," he began.

"Too bad, your interpreter is on strike." I figured he'd never understand that sentence, and I felt like getting to him somehow.

"Ah-ha, strike. Strike is something I know. Everybody in my country always on strike. Never mind. I write down words and find out meaning later." He pulled out a tiny notebook and jotted something down.

"You'll forget or misspell the words. So you'll never know."

"It is not easy to do something when you don't want to do it or are afraid. But you can do it, *ben-dodi*. Remember you have my genes."

Boy, this guy was aggravating. I leaned back against a tree. Some summer—computer camp, Color War, the boat ride, and now Pesach. It was a summer of torture, pure torture. When would it end? Then I remembered that Pesach had said something about leaving.

"Didn't you say you were going away tomorrow?"

"Yes, my friend Yoni is coming tomorrow and we will go travel a little. Washington, Boston, the Niagara great Falls. His aunt lend us a car. Why you ask? Do you want to come along?"

"No, thanks. I couldn't even if I wanted to. School

starts in another week." I was actually looking forward to school. Anything that depended on reading books, I could handle. It was much harder to terrify me in school than it was outdoors, except for gym.

"Too bad we don't have so much time anymore. But no matter. I will start you and you will work while I am gone. When I come back, you will be ready for more lessons. When I come back, I will teach you to ride bicycle. Now we must run some more." Pesach stood up and pulled me to my feet.

The guy must have hypnotized me, because I did start running. He ran alongside me, which was sort of funny since he was wearing sandals. I'd never seen anyone jog in sandals before. He slowed down a little when I started panting and gasping, and he sort of hummed some music. Then he actually started singing. The words were something like, "*Rishonim tamid anachnu.*"

Between gasps for air I asked him what he was singing.

"Very old army song, good for keeping up spirit, pace."

Maybe that song did help, or maybe it was just a little easier running with someone beside me. Anyway, I survived and we eventually made it all the way back to the car. I couldn't run that whole distance, and my cousin seemed to understand. He would run in place while I took little walking breaks to catch up to him. When we got to the car, we were both drenched with perspiration.

"*Nu?* So what do you think? See, you can do it!"

"I can't do it very well." I slumped down in the car seat. "And I don't think I could have done it without you."

"We do this again early tomorrow, before Yoni comes, and then you keep it up while I travel. Then you be ready for serious work, like bicycle. Before I go home, you will be real *gever*."

I wished he were right, but something deep inside me didn't believe it. My pathetic running was far from terrific, and I couldn't even see how becoming a better runner would help me get over being scared and worried all the time. In fact, all I could think about was how I didn't want Pesach to come back and teach me how to ride a bike. I knew I couldn't face that, and knowing it was going to happen was like knowing I was going to fall off a cliff.

I was so busy worrying that I barely remembered the party preparations we were greeted with at home. But one "Seymour, take a shower and change your clothes *immediately*" brought me back to reality.

16

FAMILY, FRIENDS, AND FLYING OBJECTS

The party was a big success. Uncles, aunts, and cousins appeared from everywhere just to meet this one Israeli guy. You'd have thought we had the celebrity of the century staying at our house, a famous athlete, or a rock star. I didn't get the attraction, but I was glad about all the company. It prevented me from being jogged around another park. Besides, the food was delicious, except for the tomatoes in the shish kebab. I can't understand who would voluntarily eat a barbecued tomato. But I got to drink soda and eat potato chips and other junk that my parents reserve for guests.

By the time everyone left, though, I was really exhausted. My parents, of course, couldn't figure out why "a young boy should be so tired" when he'd been out "sightseeing" half the day. So they made me help clean up, while Pesach was instructed to "enjoy being a guest." I thought he'd insist on helping, but he took their advice and disappeared.

"I called Bari and will go see her for a little while," he said, and winked at me. "Maybe you want to come along and visit with her little sister?"

My face felt hot. I was probably the color of one of those barbecued tomatoes.

"Are you kidding? I'd rather stay here and help my parents." It was just my luck that my cousin had met and fallen for Lari's sister. There had to be a zillion other girls in the world. What a disaster this summer had turned into!

I didn't wait up for my cousin to come home, so I was pretty rested the next day, except that getting out of bed seemed impossible. Every muscle in my body said, "Leave me alone. I can't move." So when Pesach knocked on my bedroom door, I let my muscles talk for me. "Leave me alone, please. I can't move, really."

"*Boker tov* to you too." Pesach walked right in and sat at the edge of my bed. "It feels good when muscles wake up, right? So now we give them a chance again. Come, we go run right now, before breakfast."

"You sound more like a Pharaoh than an Israeli," I moaned.

"What? Oh, Pharaoh! Good joke. I like your jokes. Now quick. Yoni could be coming sometime soon."

It was no use arguing. For every reason I gave him why I should stay in bed, he came up with two why I should get up.

"Are you going to be a lawyer, or something?" I asked when he'd finally pulled off my covers and I found myself getting dressed.

"No, I go study architecture. Come on. No more wasting time."

Pesach tried to convince me to run in our local park, and I agreed. After all, it was too early for anyone to be there and see me, and then I could avoid a long ride in the car with him.

So Pesach drove the short distance to our park, and we ran. Well, he ran, and I ran and walked again. Then it was more of that falling game, which I continued to do wrong, and finally it was home for breakfast. We walked in and found my parents sitting with a tall blond guy in brown sandals. The sandals, and the great big hugs and scream of joy that he and Pesach exchanged, told me what I'd suspected immediately. This was Yoni.

Pesach introduced me to him, and then they started babbling away in Hebrew, slapping each other on the back and laughing.

"How long has it been since you two last saw each other?" my father asked.

"Just since I came here," Pesach replied.

"You act like you've been separated for years," I commented.

"You see," Yoni said, "we have been friends since we were very young."

"Smaller than you and Ted," Pesach explained.

Ted! I'd almost forgotten all about him. He was probably furious at me over yesterday's beach mix-up. I decided I'd better try to do something about it.

"Can Ted come over, Mom? Please . . ."

"I don't see why not," she answered. "We're going to take Pesach and Yoni shopping at the mall so they can get some things they need for their trip. You'll probably have a better time doing something on your own with Ted."

I barely heard what she was saying; I was already dialing Ted. "Hi, are you busy, do you want to come over?"

"Who is this?"

"Ted, stop kidding. It's me, Seymour."

"Seymour who?"

"Me, your best friend, Seymour!"

"I do seem to remember that I did have a friend named Seymour, a long time ago."

"Okay, okay. I'm sorry. I thought Pesach was coming back and stuff. It's a long story, but it's hard to explain. Friends should accept apologies from friends."

There was silence on the other end of the line.

"I guess you're really angry," I continued. "I don't blame you. I'd have been angry in your place too. I guess I can't blame you for hating me. Bye."

I hung up the phone and glanced into the living room. They all looked so happy, and I felt so incredibly awful. The phone rang. I reached for it automatically.

"I'll be over in ten minutes, Seym." Click.

Boy, was I lucky! Ten minutes later, I was busy introducing Ted to Yoni. Ted brought over a new type of flying disk that has a dent in the middle. You spin it on your finger and then toss it in the air. He was a pro at it, and he'd just gotten it the day before! Pesach and Yoni took turns with it too. Then Yoni suggested we all go outside and have a game. I started to say, "I pulled a muscle in my arm this morning," but I was interrupted by Pesach.

"Wait. There is more to see. Let my cousin show you his computer. He can draw with it."

We all moved into my room, and Ted, Pesach, and I took turns demonstrating all the tricks that my computer drawing program can do.

"Draw a car, Seym," said Ted. "You make the best racing cars."

I was just putting in the headlights on my drawing when my parents told Yoni and Pesach they were ready to go.

Ted and I stuck around the computer a little more. Then we microwaved some pizza for lunch and told funny stories about our summers in camp.

Ted told me all about overnights and sailing and

waterskiing at his sleepaway camp. Then he told me about the time a bat flew in his bunk, and then he told about how they'd take turns telling ghost stories at night. It sounded like a lot of fun, for a normal kid, like Ted. It sounded really scary to me, except for the ghost stories. Stories don't bother me; it's only real life that keeps me scared. I thought about how far I'd have to get to ever be brave enough to go to a camp like that.

"How was your camp?" Ted asked.

"Pretty funny," I said. I told him about our computerized version of Color War.

"We have Color War, too, with team songs, and races and bonfires and great stuff. And fireworks at the end."

It sounded better than my camp's Color War, but I knew I wasn't ready for sleepaway camp. But what if Pesach's plan worked and I did get brave? Not that I saw how running every day could help. Besides, how would I run without Pesach? And Pesach was leaving.

"What ya been doing since camp?" he asked.

"Hanging out with my cousin. He calls me his tour guide. We went to the city and stuff like that." I paused. "The last couple of days we've been jogging together."

"That sounds like fun. Think I could come with you guys once, maybe?"

"Well, I'm not very good at jogging." I looked down at my toes.

"Who cares how good you are? It would be fun just to do it together. Anyway, I don't think I'm very good at jogging, either."

"Are you kidding?" I asked. "You're great at running and catching and all that stuff."

"Yeah, I'm good at most of that stuff, but I'm not sure about jogging long-distance. We had one time at camp where we had, like, a marathon, and I dropped out. It was too hard to keep going so long."

I had a feeling he was just being nice to me, but somehow I didn't care. It was more fun to run with someone, and Ted had said he didn't really care how good I was. So we made a deal to run every day until school started and then most days after school, when we could find time between all the other stuff we had to do like Hebrew school and after-school sports for Ted. I was worried that Ted might not like me when he saw how badly I ran, but somehow it was only a small worry.

Ted had to leave before my parents and Yoni and Pesach came back, so he wasn't around to see the surprise Pesach got me.

"Here," he said. "Something to keep you busy until I come back. Besides running, of course."

It was a bright yellow flying disk, just like Ted's.

"You practice on your own, throw and catch. When

I come back, we play together and do more *gever* work. When I come back you will ride bicycle."

I was enjoying trying to make that thing spin on my finger, but at the mention of the bicycle it slipped and clattered to the floor.

"When are you coming back?" I asked.

"Ten days, two weeks. I call or write, email, text. Don't worry, it won't be long."

But that's what worried me. That it wouldn't be long enough. As I waved goodbye to Yoni and my cousin, I called out, "Have a great time!" And in my heart I added, *But don't hurry back.*

17

LIFE WITHOUT PESACH

The next week went by fast. Ted and I went running every morning or every evening whenever we had time. Well, Ted went running and I went run-walk-run-walk, but there was definitely an improvement in the amount of runs versus the amount of walks, and Ted didn't make fun of me, not even once. My mom took me shopping for school clothes and school supplies, and then it was time for the first day of school.

Ted and I are never on the same bus, but we met at the front door of the school, the way we always do. We went to check the list that told us what room to go to and who our teacher was. I was shocked. For the first time in three years, Ted and I were not in the same class. Ugh! I was starting to hate school.

The bell rang, and I moped along the hall to my classroom. There were a bunch of familiar-looking faces from last year, a couple of nice kids, one bully, and oh, no, but oh, yes, there was Lari. I couldn't believe it. I was so busy staring at her that I tripped on air trying to find my seat.

"Children, do hurry and find a seat, but do it carefully, please." I heard the voice of my teacher, Mrs. Sternman. I'd heard about her from last year's fifth graders. They'd said she was stricter than strict and meaner than mean. This was not going to be a fun year. For the first time in the history of my life in school, I wished I were outside instead of in the classroom.

Mrs. Sternman wrote her name on the board. "Now we'll all go around and introduce ourselves, and then we'll all write a short paragraph or two about what we did this summer and what we expect to do this year," she said.

"Mrs. Sternman, are you going to write what you did this summer too?" asked Melanie Kips.

"I just might, dear," Mrs. Sternman answered. "Let's start with you for an introduction, young lady."

Ugh! Everybody had to say his or her name. Some people said something about themselves like "I'm Jordan, and I love the Mets." What was I going to say? I started worrying. Should I say, "I'm Seymour, and I hate my name" or "I'm Seymour, smart and scared," or better yet, "I'm Stuart Goldfarb," or maybe "Stanley Goldfarb"? This was my opportunity to be a new me, to use a better name for a better kid. Why not?

"And you, young man? We're waiting to meet you. What is your name, please?"

They were all looking at me. The teacher was talking to me. What should I say? What was my name?

Mrs. Sternman walked over to my desk. "Are you all right, son? You do know your name, don't you?"

Everyone snickered. I must have been redder than red. My cheeks felt hot. "Uh, uh, my name is St-St-St-Seymour Goldfarb." Good job, I'd lost my nerve and now the teacher would think I was a moron who thought that Seymour was spelled Steymour. This was a great start for a year. Some *gever* I was turning out to be.

Our compositions on vacation weren't much fun, either. I kept wondering what Lari wrote about camp. What if she wrote about the day I accidentally ended up in her backyard? And what if she read it out loud? That would be the end of everything.

I was perspiring as I wrote about computer camp and tried to make it sound interesting and fun. I avoided mentioning Color War and the boat ride. The teacher asked for volunteers to read what they'd written.

Some kids who'd gone to sleepaway camp volunteered, then one kid read what he'd written about his mom giving birth to twins, and another one read about a trip out West. A whole bunch of kids had written about the beach. Some kids said they hoped they'd improve in school this year or learn exciting things in math. I didn't write what I really wanted to do this year—be a different kid, a brave kid. I made up some stuff about getting to know my new classmates and learning new things too. I didn't volunteer to read my composition, and neither did Lari.

The rest of the day was spent getting books and rules and jobs and lists of stuff to buy. Somebody said that Mr. Evans, the gym teacher, had quit and taken another job. With that good news, I was starting to relax a little—until, on the way out the door at the end of the day, I suddenly heard Lari's voice.

"Did you write about your cousin?"

"Nah."

"Is he really your cousin?"

"Yeah."

"What's his name again?"

"Pesach."

"I thought that was the Hebrew word for Passover. Is it?"

"Yeah." Boy, my end of the conversation was pretty pathetic.

"I think my sister likes him."

"Oh."

"He wrote her some emails before she went to college."

"Oh."

"He said he's coming back to New York again for a little while."

"Yeah."

"Bye."

"Bye."

Wow. I had actually had a whole long conversation with Lari. Well, she had actually had half a conversation with me. Suddenly my class didn't seem so bad, except I did miss having Ted there. I was thinking of that as I sat down on the bus. At least we had a date to run together later.

Well, there were a couple of decent kids in the class, and I decided I would just stay away from Max, the bully. Mrs. Sternman didn't seem completely awful. Maybe last year's class just said she was mean so we would think they were tough. And then there was Lari. Maybe I had nothing to worry about after all.

Oh, but I did. When I got home, there was an email waiting. It included a picture of Niagara Falls.

Shalom ben-dodi,

There is a lot to see. I want to take this water home with me. We could use it. Are you running? I will be back soon. Then we will do what I promise. So be ready. Hello to parents and Ted. From Yoni too. We have mutual good time. Did I say that right?

P

I picked up my flying disk and started twirling it around. That was becoming a new habit. I wasn't good at it, but I liked it. It was soothing, and I needed to be soothed. What was I going to do? Run-walking was hard enough. There was no way I could tackle learning to ride a bike. I'd tried and failed a zillion and a half times with my dad. I couldn't do it. And I certainly didn't feel like trying and failing again in front of Pesach, or maybe even Pesach and Yoni. I would just die of embarrassment, if I didn't die of a cracked skull first from falling off.

Sometimes I wondered why everyone didn't realize how easy it was to smash your brains from falling off a bike. I'd probably known that since before I was even old enough to talk. Because she's a neurologist, my mom is always called in to fix up accident victims, so she goes crazy about potential accidents. When I was little, she bought me a helmet to wear whenever I rode my little baby bike. And that bike had no pedals; you just used your feet. Then I had a big-wheels bike and I had to wear a helmet, too, even though the big-wheels was so low to the ground it was impossible to fall off anywhere. My kind of bike!

But I had actually pedaled something once. I'd even ridden a two-wheeler with training wheels, until my father decided to loosen the back training wheels so they wobbled a little. That's when I sort of stopped riding and hung up my helmet on a hook in the garage. My dad didn't give up, though. He'd gotten me the big regular two-wheeler for my birthday a couple of years before. (My mom had gotten me a helmet to match!) But after several horrendous tries in which I ended up crying and my father ended up screaming and holding his back, the helmet wound up high on a shelf in the garage, and "my bike" became a dust collector in the garage.

I didn't want to try again. But I knew Pesach. There was no way he'd give up, not until he tried, anyway. Then he would see what a real chicken I was, and then he'd give up on me too. There had to be something I could do to prevent it, but what?

18
HELP!

It was really getting to me. I couldn't stop imagining exactly how awful it would be—Pesach coming home, trying to get me on the bike. Sometimes I pictured myself kicking and screaming and refusing to get on. Other times I imagined my whole class and Pesach and Yoni laughing as I tried to ride and fell. I daydreamed about it every day in school, and I had nightmares about it every night. It was awful. What if I came home from school and he was there, all ready and eager to teach me?

I considered, seriously considered, breaking my leg. But since fear of injuring a part of me was one of the things that kept me from riding a bike in the first place, breaking a leg seemed like a very dumb solution. I considered running away. But where could I go? Running away is not a good solution for a scared person, either. Knowing me, I'd get lost in three seconds and end up in New York City. Definitely another dumb idea.

So I switched my thoughts to Pesach. Maybe he'd get an emergency email saying they needed him urgently in Israel. Maybe Bari would come home from college and he'd be so busy with her that he'd forget me. Maybe he'd decide to stay longer in Boston, Montreal, Niagara Falls, and Washington, or wherever he was. Maybe he'd decide to go straight to California without the planned stopover back at our house. Yeah, that was a good maybe. Maybe he'd forget about teaching me to ride a bike. Maybe stranded aliens would land and ride all Earth's bikes back to outer space. I was still hoping when I came home one day and got another email. It meant he was still some-where else instead of in my house. But I went back to being scared after I read it.

Hello again, S,

Will be back Thursday or Friday. Am all set for our special lesson, ben-dodi. Get your muscles ready!

P

I felt a sense of panic, real panic, like on the boat and in the subway. What could I do?

I did what I do best. I worried. I worried from the minute I saw that email straight through Tuesday and Wednesday. By Thursday morning, I was so busy being worried that Mrs. Sternman gave me a whole lecture about daydreaming in class.

I wasn't exactly daydreaming. I was looking out the window, praying silently. *Please, God, let something help me. You could make a little rainstorm, a thunderstorm, a hurricane. These are only suggestions, you understand, but please do something.*

When I walked into the house Thursday afternoon, I was scared. But there was no sign of Pesach or Yoni. I sank back in a chair and breathed a huge sigh of relief, which felt good for about two seconds. Pesach's email had said Thursday or Friday, so that meant that I had only one day more, like some prisoner on death row who has his sentence postponed a day. Big deal!

Friday was the same as Thursday except that my sense of panic was more intense. Mrs. Sternman said she'd have to call my parents if I didn't wake up and start paying attention. I repeated my prayers for rain or any other minor disaster to help me, and when I got off the bus after school, I walked as slowly as I could to my house. But even from a distance, I saw Yoni's aunt's car. My heart was beating so fast I thought it would just pop out of my chest. I convinced myself that I might be safe as long as Yoni was around. After all, Pesach would know enough not to embarrass me in front of anyone. And if he didn't have such good sense, well, I would just tell him. "You can't teach me in front of Yoni or anyone else. That's a condition that has to be understood," I would say.

I walked up the path and opened the door. I almost tripped over the pile of suitcases, backpacks, and shopping bags in the living room. It looked as if they had just arrived and had dumped everything right by the door. So where were they?

"Pesach, Yoni?" I called out.

"Seymour?" I heard an answering voice, but it was Yoni and not Pesach who came to greet me. I guessed that maybe they'd had a rough trip with very little sleep, because he looked a mess.

"Where's Pesach?" I asked.

"In bed. He doesn't feel good."

Something about the way he said that made me think it was more than a headache. I ran to the guest room, and sure enough, Pesach was there. If I'd thought Yoni looked bad, Pesach looked ten thousand times worse. He was all drenched with perspiration.

"Pesach? Are you all right?"

"That's how you say 'welcome home'?" His voice sounded funny. "You don't even say, 'Did you have a good time, cousin?' Ow." He grimaced in pain.

"What's going on here? What's wrong with you?"

"Nothing, nothing. I must have eaten something bad at someplace. Just a stomach pain. It will . . . ow . . . go away soon."

I turned to Yoni. "How long has he been like this?"

"It started yesterday, but he wouldn't let me call a doctor. He doesn't like to go to doctors or hospitals. He wouldn't let me take him to the doctor, but he is only getting worse."

I raced out of the room and dialed my father's office. "Your father is at the hospital making rounds now, Seymour," his receptionist told me. I hung up. I tried my mother.

"She's at a staff meeting," her receptionist told me. Now what? I was panicking. Pesach was in real pain. He needed a doctor. My parents are doctors. Doctors should be disturbed in an emergency. I called back my father's receptionist. "Have him beeped, please. Tell him it's an emergency. It's my cousin, and he's sick." Then I left the same message for my mother. I decided I would call 911 for an emergency ambulance if they didn't call back in two minutes.

The phone rang. It was Ted. "I can't talk now. My cousin is sick," I said and sort of hung up on him.

The phone rang again. It was my father. "What's the matter, Son?"

The sound of his voice made me want to cry. "I didn't know what to do, Dad. It's Pesach. He came back, but he's sick. I think he's really sick. He looks awful. He's got some kind of stomach pains, and he's perspiring like crazy and moaning."

"I'm sending an ambulance. I'll meet him in the emergency room. I'll see if Mom can make it to the house."

"But, Dad, Pesach doesn't want to go to the hospital," I started to explain.

"Too bad. He has to get checked. Let me go make the arrangements." Click, back to a dial tone.

In a couple of minutes, I heard a siren, and the sound got closer. I barely had time to explain the situation to Yoni. "I called my parents. My dad sent an ambulance. Pesach has to get to the hospital."

Yoni looked really worried. "You are right, but Pesach is so stubborn. Okay. There is no choice." He ran his fingers quickly through his hair. "I should not have listened to him. It is my fault."

"It's not your fault," I called out as I raced to open the door for the ambulance attendants.

The next few minutes were a blur—Pesach lying there, protesting, then being carried out bodily on a stretcher. "But I am fine," he kept saying. "It will go away alone. No doctors."

They wouldn't let me go along in the ambulance, but Yoni took me in his car. We arrived at the hospital after the ambulance had already delivered Pesach to the emergency room. Even though I'd been to that hospital at least a zillion times with my parents, I never paid much attention to how to get there, so my directions weren't the greatest.

I think I was also confused because I was really, really nervous. When we finally raced into the emergency room, I asked a nurse if she'd seen either Dr. Judy Goldfarb or Dr. David Goldfarb.

"They are both in with a patient," she replied.

"But they're my parents, and that patient is my cousin!" I was practically screaming. "I have to talk to them, to see them, right away. It's an emergency."

The nurse stood up. "Of course it's an emergency. This is the emergency room. Calm down. We can't allow hysterics in the lobby, even from a doctor's son. Have something to drink. There's a soda machine over there. I'll see what I can do."

I didn't want soda. I just wanted to know how Pesach was. Yoni seemed to be in the same state. He was pacing up and down that tiny lobby, and he kept running his fingers through his hair angrily or banging one fist into his other open hand.

After what seemed like years, my mother finally came out of the doors marked NO ADMITTANCE. She looked like a regular doctor, in a green surgical uniform and all, but to me she was just my mom. I ran to her and buried my head against her. I felt the tears surging through me, and I lost the battle to keep them inside. I was blubbering and sobbing like a baby.

"Now, calm down. Crying isn't going to help," she

said, but she sounded pretty choked up herself. "Where's Yoni?"

Yoni walked over sheepishly and joined us.

"Don't be so down, the two of you. It was a good thing you called when you did. It's his appendix. It's ruptured, but Pesach is in the hands of our best surgeon and he'll be fine, just fine."

"I don't understand." Yoni looked up at my mother. She explained about the appendix and how it had burst.

"But he could get very sick from that, no?" Yoni asked.

My mother seemed to stiffen slightly. "Who is the doctor here, anyway?" she said brightly. "I don't want either of you two worrying. Pesach will be fine. He's in the hospital. He is undergoing surgery as we speak. Now go on home, both of you."

"But can't we see him? We'll wait till he comes out of the operating room, Mom," I begged.

"That won't be so soon," she said, stroking my head. "And then he'll be in the recovery room for a while. Either your father or I will stay with him. I promise." She turned to Yoni. "And you will stay with us, of course." It sounded more like an order than an invitation.

"No, thank you, Mrs.—I mean, Dr.—Goldfarb. My aunt is expecting me. I promised to give her the car back."

"Why don't you call her?"

"No, I will go. She will worry. And my family has planned a party for me tomorrow." That sounded familiar. "I will call you tonight. I will take Seymour home. Do you want that I should stay with him till you come home?"

"No, he'll be fine. Seymour, maybe Ted can come over till one of us gets home. What do you think?"

"I want to stay here until I know he's okay. I have to stay here. I have to," I pleaded.

"No, an emergency room lobby is no place for a young boy, even for my son!" She was trying to sound cheery. "So off with the both of you now. Your father or I will be home soon. I will call you as soon as Pesach comes out of surgery, I promise."

Yoni and I were soon in the car again on the way home. We were both silent. I was trying not to cry. Yoni was concentrating on the road, but every time we hit a red light or a stop sign, he'd brush his hair back again or kind of hit the steering wheel.

"I think my things are still at your place," Yoni said suddenly when we pulled up in front of the house. "When we came here, I was very worried about Pesach. He tried to bring in suitcases. I said I would do it, and I was so nervous I brought mine in too. I should have taken him to doctor yesterday, even if he didn't want to go. It is all my fault."

"No, it isn't, Yoni, really it isn't." I knew it wasn't his fault at all. It was my fault, all completely and totally my fault. I was the one who'd been so selfishly worried about learning to ride a bicycle that I'd prayed for something to prevent it. I hadn't meant something like this. Rain was what I'd meant. But rain wasn't what I got. I couldn't explain all this to Yoni. I couldn't explain it to anyone.

19

SURGERY AND SUFFERING

Boy, that was some awful night. Ted called to find out what had happened to my cousin. Somehow I managed to tell him about the ambulance and the operation. I guess I didn't sound too good. He came over to wait until my parents came home, even though his mother suggested that I stay with them for the rest of the day. I told them I didn't want to leave the house. My mom had promised to call, so I was going to stick as close as possible to the telephone. I kept staring at that dumb phone, waiting for it to ring. And every time it rang, I jumped. Once it was a wrong number, once it was for my mother, and once it was Yoni.

Ted brought over pizza, and I don't even remember if I ate it or not. I just remember staring at that phone and feeling awful. I couldn't tell Ted it was my fault; I couldn't even tell my parents. It was a private problem, too terrible to talk about.

My mom finally called and said the surgery was over and "there's nothing for you to worry about." I tried to believe her, but I had a feeling that I wouldn't stop worrying until I actually saw Pesach get out of there.

Ted just sort of hung out, trying to get me interested in the computer, the television, or anything. But it was no use.

My mom finally came home, and then Ted's mom came to take him home. My mother looked exhausted.

"Your father will stay in the hospital for a couple of hours more, and then I'll go there and he'll come home. That way when Pesach wakes up, at least he'll see a familiar face."

I was glad the face he saw wouldn't be mine. I was the one who'd gone and done this to him.

I can't remember much else about that night. After Mom called Yoni, she insisted that I go to sleep. But that wasn't the easiest thing to do. I had trouble falling asleep, and then I dreamed that I visited Pesach in the hospital and that he was hooked up to tubes and wires and machines and that the doctors and nurses were all standing around the bed looking worried. In the dream I called out, "I didn't mean it! I didn't mean it!" I woke up and realized that this was one dream that was just as real as real life, unfortunately.

I lay there in my bed, in the dark, and thought. I thought of my poor cousin in pain and misery. I felt so mean, so stupid, and so guilty. Then I remembered what Yoni had asked: if the ruptured appendix might be dangerous. Could Pesach really be seriously, critically ill? I jumped out of bed. I'd heard something. It was my father's car.

I opened the door of my room a crack and heard my parents talking. They said something about "peritonitis," and then my mom left for the hospital. I opened the door and went out to see my dad.

"Seymour." He whirled around when he heard me come into the room. "Do you know what time it is? Why are you up?"

"I can't sleep, Dad. I'm worried about Pesach. What's peritonitis?" I asked.

"Where did you . . . ?" He sat down on the sofa. "Come sit next to me, Son." He patted the seat next to him and waited until I sat down before he went on. "Peritonitis is a kind of poisoning that sometimes happens when an appendix bursts, when it isn't caught before it ruptures," he explained.

"Can you die from that?"

"You can die from anything! You could choke on a chocolate chip cookie," he said, trying hard to be funny.

"Really, Dad."

"Really, Seymour."

"Will he die? He can't die. I didn't mean for him to die."

"Stop babbling like a nincompoop! He's going to be fine. Oh, he'll have some pain for quite a few days, but he'll be fine."

"Are you sure?"

"I'm sure that it's way past your bedtime. Now get to bed immediately, and I'm going to do the exact same thing. That way when your mother comes back, I'll have enough energy to go back there myself."

"Do I have to go with you to see him?"

"Don't you want to?" He looked at me for a minute. "He won't be up to visitors for a while, and children under sixteen are really not supposed to be up there on the surgical ward at all. But your mother and I have a little pull. We might ask them to bend the rules a little so that you can see him. And I'm sure he'll want to see you."

He wouldn't want to ever see me if he knew the truth. I knew that.

"You shouldn't ask for special privileges just because you're doctors," I volunteered.

"Sometimes you are impossible to understand," answered my father. "I would have thought you'd be dying to see him."

"Good night, Dad. I am tired."

I hoped that things would look better in the morning. They didn't. My father wasn't home, and my mother was sleeping. She'd left me a note that Pesach was improving and that I might be able to call him later. I moped around the house, did some homework, and felt awful.

Ted called and wanted to run. Yoni called and asked me about Pesach and wanted to talk to one of my parents. I promised him that one of them would call him back as soon as possible.

When my father finally came home, he said Pesach was doing a little better. "I had to call his mother, and, of course, she was worried. In fact, she wanted to get on the next plane. But I convinced her that there was no need."

"Is Pesach awake?" I asked.

"On and off. He's pretty heavily sedated."

"Did he mention me?"

"He hasn't said anything yet, actually; he's mostly listened."

And with that, he went to sleep. I tried to read, one of my favorite things, ordinarily. Then I went to one of my father's medical texts and tried reading about appendicitis and peritonitis. It was pretty technical stuff. I kept searching through the medical books, trying to get some understandable information from each. Peritonitis didn't sound so hot, but at least it seemed that there were things you could do to combat it. That made me feel a little better.

I had a brainstorm. I'd make Pesach a get-well card on the computer. He was crazy about my drawing program. So I made him a card with a picture of a big running shoe.

Dear Pesach,

Hope you'll soon be up and running!

From,
Your madrich

Maybe if I send him cards every day, I won't have to face him in person, I thought as I printed out the card. So I sat down to try to plan some more cards. The sound of the telephone interrupted me. It was Yoni.

"Oh, Seymour, how are you? What is new? I have not slept all night. Is he okay? Do you want me to call his family in Israel? When can I visit him?"

"Hold on, Yoni! You aren't leaving me any time to answer. My folks took turns staying in the hospital and were with Pesach all night. They already called his parents, and they say he's going to be fine." I didn't mention that I heard that they'd been worried about peritonitis. Yoni was worried enough.

"I will come tomorrow to visit him and you. It is only one-hour drive. I can do it. I must do it. If I had made him go to doctor before, his appendix would not have, uh, exploded."

"Stop blaming yourself!" I tried not to scream. "I know it isn't your fault, and I'm sure he knows it. So just stop thinking like that. Hey, give me your phone number again so my parents can call you." I wasn't exactly eager to continue this conversation. I jotted down the phone number, even though I already had it, and said goodbye.

The phone rang again the instant I put the receiver down.

It was Ted. He invited me to go to the movies with him and his little brother. I jumped at the chance. I was a little worried about leaving without asking my parents' permission, but I figured that waking them up might be worse. So I left them five identical notes to be sure they'd spot at least one, and I left them all over in strategic spots: on the kitchen table, on the phone, on top of the toilet, by the door, and in the refrigerator.

The movie was hilarious. It was about two guys who are on a flight to Europe, but they fall asleep on the plane and end up in the desert somewhere. Ted and I were laughing so hard we knocked over our popcorn. Ted's little brother kept saying, "I don't get it. What's so funny?" Every time he asked that, Ted or I tried to explain, but we'd crack up laughing in the middle.

It sure felt good to laugh. When we walked out of that dark theater, I felt better than I had in days. But when the sunlight hit my eyes, I remembered that my troubles were far from over. Pesach was still in the hospital. I was still a scared baby, so scared of riding a bike that I'd ended up accidentally wishing Pesach sick. Ugh!

Ted's mom picked us up and said my parents had phoned her after reading at least one of my notes. They were delighted that I was busy, and they were already back at the hospital. They left a number for me to call.

I did call from Ted's house, and a woman's voice answered, "Room 324."

"Is Dr. Goldfarb there?"

"Which Dr. Goldfarb did you want?"

"Either one, I'm their son."

"Oh, the Goldfarbs' son, how nice. Well, neither one is here right now. I'm the nurse they hired to look after their, I mean your, cousin. Just a minute." There was a pause. "Your cousin overheard our conversation. He'd like to talk to you."

"But, no, I don't want to bother him," I started to protest.

"You no bother me." I recognized Pesach's accent, but his voice sounded so far away. "You come see me soon, we talk real, no phone, *ben-dodi*?"

"Sure, sure. You just get better."

"Come soon."

"Yeah, in a few days."

The nurse got back on the phone, and I left a message for my folks. "Say I'm still at Ted's." I had to talk loudly 'cause Ted's older brother was back, and they were wrestling on the floor. I couldn't tell if they were really fighting or fooling around. Soon their little brother had joined in the fighting, and then their mother was there breaking it up. I wondered what it was like to have a brother, or two like Ted did.

When my mother called back, Ted's mom invited me to sleep over. Ted and I started jumping up and down. "Say yes, say yes," we mouthed. And unbelievably, she did. She said that either she or my dad would come by later to drop off a change of clothes and things for me. I knew she'd do that—my folks think your teeth will fall out if you miss a day's brushing, so they would have come just to bring me my toothbrush!

When my dad came by, he said that Pesach was much better and that maybe I could visit him the next day, Sunday.

"I know you really want to see him," he said as he gave me a fatherly parting hug.

I did want to see him, but through a one-way mirror so that I could see him without him seeing me.

I had trouble falling asleep in Ted's house, though for some reason I'm not exactly afraid of sleeping over there, maybe because I've done it already. I remember that I was scared the first time. I worried about the color of my pajamas. Maybe other kids didn't wear pajamas? I worried about suddenly snoring or talking in my sleep or something else gross that would make Ted decide that I was a major disaster. But I'd survived that first time, and besides, I loved having Ted sleep over, and it wasn't fair for him always to sleep at my house. That's how my mother had talked me into sleeping at his house that first time, when I'd been almost too scared to go.

Still, though it wasn't the first time or the second or even the fifth time staying over at Ted's, it felt weird sleeping in a different bed, looking at different wallpaper. I looked up at the bed on top of me and wondered what would happen if it suddenly collapsed and fell. Ted always offered to let me sleep on the top bunk, but I have enough trouble worrying about falling when I'm flat on the ground. Maybe it was safer to be on the top bunk after all.

Boy, I have to quit worrying like this, I reminded myself. Look at all the trouble I'd already gotten myself into. Maybe I should tell Ted about it, I thought: confide in him, start at the beginning about the bike and being afraid and hoping that Pesach wouldn't try to teach me. It was too embarrassing. Still, I needed advice.

"Ted," I whispered softly. But Ted didn't answer. He was already asleep. So I had to keep my problem to myself—which was probably not such a bad idea anyway.

20

FACE TO FACE

Of course, I did have to go to see Pesach eventually, but I didn't expect it to be so soon. The next day, when my parents picked me up, they drove me straight to the hospital. They told me that they'd arranged special clearance for me to visit my cousin.

"Aren't you glad we're doctors?" my mother asked cheerily. "You know that children aren't usually allowed to visit up on the surgical ward."

"Maybe there's a good reason why children aren't allowed up there." I figured one last valiant try might still save me.

"Come on, hurry up, Sy. You have to wear this mask." My father wasn't listening to me, for a change.

So there I was, suddenly walking through those hospital corridors, past nurses and patients and wheelchairs and stretchers and right into a room marked 324.

There were two beds in there. The guy in the first bed looked about 150 years old, and his face was full of prickly stubble that was practically long enough to turn into a beard. I was so nervous that I actually approached that bed and said, "Pesach, is that you? You look great."

My mom and dad cracked up laughing, and the patient in the next bed made a sound that sounded like a laugh that was trying to come out of a box with a tight lid on it.

"Please no more jokes yet, *ben-dodi*. It hurts too much to laugh."

There he was, looking mostly like the way he should have looked except a little scraggly and maybe a little skinny or just a little tired.

"I like the card that you made for me," he continued. "Are you still running?"

I just stood silently, looking at him.

"Hello, are you under that mask, *ben-dodi*?" he asked when I still hadn't said anything.

"Yeah, sure, I'm here."

"So sit down a minute. Have a drink from my pitcher of water. It's the best food around here."

"When patients start complaining about the food, it's a sign they want to leave," my father said as he put his arm around me.

"So can I leave?" Pesach asked.

"Boy, are you in a hurry." My mom laughed. "Not so fast, I'm afraid. But it shouldn't be too long."

"You must make them tell me how soon." Pesach looked at me imploringly. "It's not too much fun in here.

I like your house better, the food, too, and the company."
He winked at me.

My parents walked out the door for a minute. I sat
down and tried not to look at the guy in the other bed,
who was now snoring with his mouth open, or at the
charts by the foot of the bed or at the bedpans. But there
really wasn't anything else to look at. No words seemed
to be coming out of my mouth.

"I guess you are like me," Pesach volunteered. "Even
though your parents are doctors, you do not seem too
happy to be in hospital. Not me also." He seemed to be
waiting for me to say something. I said nothing.

"You are angry at me. How you say, disappointed in
me? I understand."

"What are you talking about?" I seemed to suddenly
wake up.

"Because I tell you I will make you *gever* and then you
see that I am not all brave, not all *gever* myself. It's true, no?"

"No! I don't know what you're talking about." And
I really didn't.

"You do not have to worry about hurting my feelings. I cannot do much yet but lie in bed, so I have had
time to think. I know how you feel."

"No, Pesach," I interrupted. "You don't know anything!"

"See! I knew that is how you would feel. Now that you
have seen that I, too, am afraid, you no longer trust in me."

"What?" I jumped up. What was he talking about?

"You saw that I am, well, afraid maybe of going to doctors and hospital. That is why I wait too long, not let Yoni take me. Have what you call ripped appendix."

"Ruptured appendix."

"Same thing. You understand?"

"I didn't know you were afraid. That's not what happened," I tried to explain.

"But it is true. And it is good that I tell you. So now you know that every person is afraid of something, see? You are a little afraid of some things, and now maybe you see that even I am afraid, once in my life, at least." He smiled. "I am sorry that I, how you say, disappoint you, not teach you, and be poor example myself. I do not blame you for being angry."

"But I'm not angry," I blurted out. "You are the one who should be angry. I'll never be a *gever*."

"You can be whatever you want to be. You can do it."

A sudden noise at the door and a blabbering of Hebrew announced the arrival of Yoni, followed almost immediately by my parents, who pronounced my visit over.

I left the building kind of shaken up. So Pesach, too, had been afraid of something, and it had almost killed him! I made up my mind right then and there to do something to get over my fears. I'd turn myself into a *gever* somehow. The only question was, How?

21

THANK GOODNESS FOR BEES

Little did I know that Mrs. Sternman would help me in my project to become brave, or at least braver. Well, she didn't know she was helping me, but she was. Mrs. Sternman started teaching us about how to do research in the library. This year we were learning advanced things, like how to use search engines to explore the internet responsibly.

"Everyone uses 'google' as a verb," she said. "But Google is a search engine, and there are others, too. You can use any or all of these to find information. But did you know you have to reference what you find to make sure it's true?"

Mrs. Sternman and the librarian used the whiteboard to demonstrate searching on more than one search engine site. "Pay attention to the URL of the site, and copy and paste that into your bibliography when you use internet research."

"Tonight's homework will be to go to a library or use the school library or a computer at home. Use at least two search engines to come up with an interesting fact about an animal, any animal that you choose. Remember, try to find an interesting fact and support it with information from at least two sources. It would be ideal if your sources came from more than one search engine," she said.

The librarian and Mrs. Sternman moved among us to be sure we knew how to search and recognize the URL information as a site to copy as a reference. It was kind of fun because, of course, I love computers.

The librarian said we could phrase a question in the search box instead of just typing in a topic name. "For instance, you could type in 'How big is an ostrich's egg?' to find specific information about one of the most interesting facts about an ostrich."

We worked in pairs and typed that in and came up with all kinds of other suggestions of things to look up, like 'How big is an ostrich's eye? How big is an ostrich's brain? How strong is an ostrich's egg?'

It was fun. I started thinking about what animal I would look up for homework and what question I could look up about that animal.

By the time I was home, sitting in front of the computer, I had a few ideas about which animal to investigate. Camels interest me. So do armadillos. But I suddenly had a great idea for a question. What animal is so big that it probably isn't afraid of anything? An elephant.

I went to Google and typed, "What are elephants afraid of?"

I expected the answer to be "Unlike Seymour J. Goldfarb, who is afraid of everything, elephants are never afraid."

There were a couple of articles about elephants being afraid. One said they were afraid of ants that lived in an acacia tree. Another article said they were afraid of bees. It even said how scientists can use that fear to keep the elephants away from people's crops.

Next, I checked out Bing with the same questions. There was a different article about elephants and their fears. Bees. "Elephants are afraid of bees," it said.

It sort of astonished me that elephants might be afraid of bees. Maybe it was thinking about bees that made me think of the letter *b*, which is also the first letter of the word *bicycle,* or maybe I just had my own fear on my mind. I decided to try a new search.

In the search box, I typed, "afraid to ride a bike." Within seconds, there was a flood of suggested articles. *The Easy Way to Learn to Ride; No Pain Learning to Ride; Teach Your Child the Foolproof Way.* There were even some videos. One showed a kid so young that he was probably in kindergarten. I watched the videos and read the articles. They made it sound simple.

"Make sure the child can reach the ground when

sitting on the bicycle seat. Then have him walk the bike until that feels comfortable. Gradually, your child will be able to lift one foot and then the other, developing a sense of balance and trust on his own, at his own pace, until one day he will just ride."

I wanted to believe it was possible. The videos showed lots of kids doing it, kids much younger than me even. It was worth a try. I printed out one of the articles and stuffed it into my pocket.

Five minutes after reading the articles and watching the videos, I had it all planned. I'd go in the garage, check out the bike, and start immediately.

The garage did not disappoint. There was the bike, all dusty and cobwebby, looking just as it was: something unwanted.

"Don't worry, Bike, I have come to save you—and me, I might add."

Cleaning it up was a little gross, but there was no other way, and at last I was ready to attempt sitting on it, to see if I could reach the floor. There wasn't a whole lot of room in the garage, what with all the lawn furniture and gardening tools and my father's bicycle and assorted boxes that my parents have stored there. But actually that made me feel safer; I had lots to hold on to while getting ready just to sit on my old enemy.

My feet reached easily. I guess, short as I am, I still

must have grown some since the last time my father tried me on that thing. Great, one problem down and only the learning-to-ride part left.

But there was no room to try out my system in the garage, and I certainly couldn't take the bike outside in front of the house for all the world to see what a moron I still was. This plan was more complicated than it had first appeared.

I glanced at the printout again: "Take the bicycle somewhere where there is room to ride and, of course, no danger of cars," it said.

There was nowhere I could take it that I could be sure of not being seen, and how would I get it there even if there was such a place? Carry it on my shoulders, up and down the streets of Long Island?

"That's it, Bike! I'll take you down, downstairs in the basement. No cars there, ha, ha!"

I don't know how I managed it. Getting it down the basement steps wasn't simple, and I was drenched in per-spiration by the time I did it. But at last there we were, alone together in a place where no one could see what was going on.

I put the bike near the wall and sat on it again, with the kickstand down, just to play it safe. "Tomorrow we'll ride!" I announced cheerfully.

22

PRACTICE MAKES PERFECT?

Life is simpler on the internet than it is in real life. The next day I discovered that my bicycle wouldn't move. One of the tires was sort of squashed flat. Luckily, my father had an old bike pump, and after I searched for the instruction manual (my father always keeps those) and after a zillion tries, I finally got some air in the tire. I guess it sort of helped that I'd seen Pesach try to fix Bari's bicycle. But it still took me a while to get the thing full of air.

So there went one more afternoon down the drain. I couldn't spend all my time downstairs in the basement without my parents coming down to look for me, so I did what I could between when I got home from school and they got home from work.

It was slow going. But I was eventually brave enough to release the kickstand and walk it around the basement. I sat on the bike and walked and walked and walked until beads of sweat were pouring down my head, and I was almost as wet as from running.

Running. There wasn't enough time in the afternoon to run with Ted. I'd have to tell Ted that I'd pulled a muscle so that I'd have time to work on the bike. Besides, I didn't have enough physical energy to do both. I didn't like telling Ted another dumb scaredy-cat-type excuse, but then again, there didn't seem to be a whole lot of choice. If I said, "Ted, I can't go running this week because I'm busy in my basement, teaching myself how to ride a bicycle," Ted would have thought I was crazy.

But when I did call Ted, he acted funny. If I didn't know better, I'd have thought that he suspected something. I don't think I said anything that could have made him suspicious. I just called him up and said, "Hey, Ted, I think I pulled a muscle in my leg. It's pretty painful. I'd better not go running for a week or two. We'll start again as soon as it's better. I don't think it should take more than two weeks." Ted was silent for a few seconds, and then he acted a little weird.

"Did you say you pulled a muscle, Seym?"

"Yeah, in my leg."

"When?" he shot back.

"Uh, I don't know when. It must have been Sunday. I think maybe I didn't stretch enough before we went running, but of course it could have happened just getting out of bed, right? You know how these things are."

"Yeah, I know," he said, but it sounded more like "Yeah, I know what you're up to." Then he said something even stranger. "Seym, we're good friends, right?"

"Yeah, I'd say best friends was the same or better than good friends, Ted. I always thought we were best friends."

"That's what I thought, too, Seym. I really did."

"Well, we are, Ted." He didn't say anything. I started thinking that maybe he liked running even more than I did. Maybe he was, like, addicted to it or something. "I'm not quitting running, Ted, if that's what you think. Honest. This is just temporary, a break, because of my leg, the muscle you know. Okay? You're not angry or anything, are you?"

"Why should I be angry?" Ted asked, but he didn't sound non-angry to me. "I mean, if you can't tell a friend what's bothering you, what's a friend for? That's what I think."

I didn't spend much time thinking about what he meant. I didn't have too much time or energy left for anything but trying to master that bike. I was determined to do it before Pesach came home from the hospital.

A couple of times my parents took me to the hospital to see him. I brought Pesach my flying disk and told him to keep twirling it in bed, on one finger. He liked the idea. My parents had managed to get him some books in Hebrew as well as some magazines and things to read, and of course there was television.

Every time I saw him, he mentioned how eager he

was to get out of there, and I can't say I blamed him. I just hoped I'd learn to ride before he got home.

Between visiting Pesach, doing my regular schoolwork, and walking around the basement on that dumb bicycle, I was busy every minute of the day. After a few days, walking on the bicycle was pretty easy, and I even lifted up first one foot and then the other for a few seconds, but I still wasn't riding. I reread that folded-up article so many times that I was afraid it would tear from overuse by sweaty hands.

"When the child has mastered walking, tell him to glide, sort of using the foot to propel him forward as if he were on a scooter," the article said.

Ted had a scooter, and I'd seen him scoot. I'd never felt like trying it myself. I closed my eyes and tried to picture the gliding movement they meant.

I tried and tried until I think I sort of did it right. I pushed off with both feet until it zoomed a little forward, and then I quickly put my feet back on the ground and did it again and again. The only problem was the basement was not exactly big enough to really move. I kept trying not to crash into the washer and dryer and the poles in the basement. It was tricky. And one night I almost forgot to camouflage the bike before I went upstairs. Imagine what would have happened if one of my parents had come down to do laundry and found the bike?

At least I was no longer terrified of the bike, and we were kind of getting across the room together somehow with me still in an upright position. But it wasn't exactly what a normal person would call riding a bike. I finally realized that I had made about as much progress as a person could make indoors. I would have to do the same thing but outside.

When could I practice riding outside without being seen? After school, when there were mothers and kids and stuff around? When everyone was in school, I was in school too. That's when I realized it would have to be before school, before my parents got up and before life in our neighborhood got going. I ran upstairs and checked the paper: sunrise was real early. That's it! I thought. I'd get up with the sun, ride around a little, and come back in before anyone else was up. Brilliant idea!

23

OUTSIDE

Me and my brilliant ideas! First, I had to drag that bike all the way upstairs again, which seemed even harder than it had been getting it down there in the first place. Then I had to set the alarm clock for the crack of dawn and turn it off the second it rang so that I wouldn't wake my parents up.

But the worst thing was, I had to get up when it rang. Ugh! Getting up that early was tough. Quietly, I tiptoed outside and then went for the bicycle. Did you ever try to open a garage door without making a sound? I don't think it's possible. I tried opening it ever so slowly the first day and then really fast the second day, but both days it made a horrendous noise. But I did it and my parents didn't wake up.

Just to be on the safe side, I'd decided to bring along my new, never-been-worn eyeglasses. My parents always drag me around for annual checkups (dentist, pediatrician, and eye doctor). The eye doctor had prescribed glasses "to be worn if you feel you need them for the blackboard or movies, Seymour." The glasses would be a perfect disguise. Since I hadn't started wearing them yet, no one would recognize me with them on! So if anyone did spot me on my be-a-*gever* workout, I could pretend to be someone else who just happened to look like me. (Besides, since I was going to be in the street, where a car might suddenly appear, it might not hurt to have perfect vision on my side.)

Glasses on, I climbed on the bike and practiced just the same steps I'd practiced in the basement. And then, that second morning, I was gliding and lifting and gliding and lifting when suddenly both my feet were up in the air at the very same moment and I didn't fall and I put my feet on the pedals and they moved slowly around and around and the wheels turned and the bike moved and I was riding! I, Seymour J. Goldfarb, was gliding up and down the block. Okay, so at the end of the block, I had to get off and turn the bike around and then get back on again because I didn't know how to turn yet. But it felt so amazing, so incredible; I just wanted to do it over and over, all day long.

I felt terrific, like I guess somebody feels when they win a contest or get a trophy or something else equally stupendous. I wanted to shout, "I am a *gever*! No more *pachdan*! Hey, world, move over, here comes Seymour J. Goldfarb, ex-*pachdan*, ex-chicken, potential future Olympic bicycling champion!"

But I didn't shout. I didn't even whisper. I didn't tell a soul, not Pesach or my parents or Ted—no one. I just kept my secret. I wanted Pesach to be the first to know, and I didn't want to tell him, I wanted to show him. Besides, I was still rather wobbly on my new wheels, and I didn't want to show anyone that I could do it, but badly. But I think I deserve some kind of award or something for keeping it a secret. I felt like the news was going to burst out of me and splatter all over the place.

I thought about writing to the people who'd posted the articles on the internet. I figured I owed them a lot and I should write thank-you emails, if I got up the nerve and if there was a way to find the people who'd written those articles. More search engine challenges, but I could probably figure out how to find those authors.

The other person I owed was my cousin. He sort of inspired me, I guess. And I owed him plenty to make up for sort of getting him into the hospital with my dumb fears.

I still couldn't believe it was true. I, Seymour J. Goldfarb, could now ride a normal, regular, two-wheel-type, formerly scary bike. Maybe I wouldn't even have to change my name.

24

PATIENCE FOR THE PATIENT

Pesach was finally released from the hospital. We had major preparations going on for his homecoming. I made a million computerized banners welcoming him home. My mom and Ted and I blew up a ton of balloons, all blue and white for Israel.

Ted's mom baked a big cake. Ted and I helped her by licking the bowl and the beaters. Yoni was at our house, too, helping us hang up the balloons, when Bari called. It seemed that she'd been calling and emailing Pesach all along.

At last Pesach came in, twirling the flying disk in one hand. He looked a little skinnier than I think he was before, but he still seemed to be full of fun and jokes. He showed me and Ted some cool twirling moves that he'd mastered while bedridden in the hospital. And he made us all laugh telling us all the new English words he'd learned in the hospital, like *bedpan*, *needle*, *painkiller*, and *stitches*.

At last everyone was gone. Yoni left to go cross-country, the trip Pesach would have gone on if not for his appendix. Ted went home, my mom went to the hospital to check on some patients, and my father went into the kitchen to clean up.

I was bursting to tell Pesach what I'd done, or rather what I could do. I couldn't wait to see his face, watching me ride my bike.

"How about—" I began.

"Pesach, it's time for some rest—doctor's orders," said my father from the doorway, still wearing an apron and carrying a dishtowel. "I promised your surgeon that we'd take good care of you. And I promised your mother too!"

"I guess I am a little tired," Pesach said.

"But wait. I've got to . . . can't he just . . ." I wasn't sure how to explain without giving myself away.

"You'll have lots of time to spend with Pesach, Seymour, before he can get up and around and back to his sightseeing. But we don't want to tire him out and certainly not on his first night home from the hospital, right?"

"Right."

Boy, was I disappointed! Pesach went to bed, and I went to mope. All that waiting for him to come home and see the great Seymour-biking performance, and now I had to wait some more.

I tried to convince myself that this delay would just mean I'd be one day better at riding. Since I wasn't able to show off that day, I decided that I might as well continue my crack-of-dawn practicing. Then I'd really be good when I showed Pesach. Yes, that's what I'd do.

So that next morning, I crawled out of bed quietly and put on my glasses, just as I had been doing for the last few days. As noiselessly as possible, I opened the garage and started my morning ride. Once to the end of the block, get off, turn around, back to my house, and then the same thing over again a couple of times. Then I retraced my steps back through the garage, opened the door that led from the garage to the kitchen, and bumped right into Pesach—the smilingest Pesach I'd ever seen.

"I heard noises, got up, and heard garage door, so I look out window and what do I see, my *madrich* is *gever* already on the bicycle. *Mazel tov, ben-dodi*. I am very proud. Who taught you?"

We sat in the kitchen and had a celebration breakfast while I told him everything about the articles and practicing in the basement. I explained about the eyeglasses too. He held his side and winced in pain, trying not to laugh.

"This is best story. How you say, a do-it-yourself job, right? So what do your parents say? And Ted? They are proud, too, no?"

"No. I mean, it's not that they aren't proud. I mean they don't know. I haven't shown anyone yet. I'm still kind of a beginner. I can't even turn around without getting off and turning the bike around. And I have to place the pedals in just a certain way to get going. I thought I'd show them when I look like a normal person."

Pesach really laughed then. It was a weird sound, a combination "ha, ha" mixed with an "oy vey" from laughing where it hurt. It was such a funny sound that it made me start laughing too.

That's how my parents found us, and we just laughed harder and harder every time they asked us if we could please explain what great joke had us up and laughing so early. Pesach didn't give me away; he just winked at me.

25
WHO KNOWS?

Pesach leaves next week. He's pretty well recuperated, and he's got to get home for his "studies," as he calls it. Since he came home from the hospital, he's rested a lot and acted as my coach, telling me what to do on the bike so that now I can even turn around. He'd get up with me before school and then go outside with me after school as my own personal cheerleader.

I'm planning on showing my parents this week. I can't wait to see their faces, and I promised Pesach that I'd show them before he leaves for Israel. And I've already dropped a hint to Ted. We started running again, and while we were out there panting I said, "You know, this isn't bad, but I read somewhere that you're supposed to give your muscles a rest by doing alternate activities. You know, one day running, next day swimming or something."

"Did I hear you say you want to go swimming?" Ted started choking with laughter.

"That's not what I meant, but I don't see what's so funny, anyway. No, I uh, I uh, I uh, thought that maybe we could do one day running, next day biking. What do you think?"

Ted stopped short. You're not supposed to do that when you're running; you're supposed to slow down gradually. I don't know what got into him. He just whirled around and stared at me like he'd never seen me before.

"Seymour, I think I'm hearing things. What did you say?"

"Keep running," I said, pulling him. "It's not healthy to stop like that."

"But I couldn't hear you clearly! I didn't think that you c . . . uh, did, I mean, liked bike riding."

I was going to say something like, "Well, my cousin helped me fix my bike, you know the one that always had a flat tire," but I couldn't say it. I figured that I didn't have anything to cover up anymore about bikes. And Ted was, is, my best friend. So I just said, "Yeah, well, I guess running has changed me or something. 'Cause now I'm thinking of riding bikes with you someday soon. A little, of course, not too far, not near traffic or anything."

Ted started jumping up and down then. He acted really happy, and he was kind of muttering to himself. If I didn't know that it was impossible, I'd have thought that he'd figured the whole thing out. But I was sure he couldn't have, 100 percent sure—well, maybe 95 percent sure. The happier he seemed, the less sure I was.

"That's a great idea, Seym," he said suddenly. "A truly great idea. Maybe even brilliant. We'll jog and we'll ride bikes sometimes. And don't worry, we'll stay away from cars for a while until you get used to it, I mean, until we get used to riding together and all. So when do you want to start?"

I told him that maybe we should wait until my cousin left. I wanted to spend a lot of time with him while he was still nearby.

I told Pesach about Ted's reaction to my suggestion that we go bike riding. "It almost seemed as if he knew I was afraid before," I said. "Though that's impossible."

"Ted is a good friend, a true *chaver*," he said. "Not every friend is a *chaver*."

"But we learned in Hebrew school that *chaver* means 'friend,'" I told him, "so how could a friend not be a *chaver*? Don't tell me English is the only confusing language."

"Not confusing at all. We have two words for friends. The other one is for someone who is friend but not special, true good friend. That other kind is *yedid*. *Yedid* is good, too, easier to find. We can have many *yedidim* but not many *chaverim*. *Chaverim* are harder to find and harder to keep."

I tried to think of an English word for *yedid*. I guess it's kind of like an acquaintance, or maybe there is no word for it. But I know that Pesach is right about Ted's being the other kind of friend, the better one.

Pesach and I had time for some long talks again. He says it's not good to pretend, like I used to. "You should not hide who you really are," he says, and something like, "It's good to be yourself but is also good to constantly aim higher."

"I shall try to like hospitals more," he promised.

"And I shall try to conquer a few more of my fears," I promised. "But how will I get braver without your help?"

"You are your best friend. You will help you."

"What does that mean?" I asked.

"There is famous Hebrew saying, '*Im ain ani li, mi li?*' which means 'If I am not for myself, who will be for me?'" Pesach continued.

"I still don't get it," I answered.

"You are the one who wanted to learn to ride that bike, and you are the one who did it, you see?"

"I guess I do, a little."

"But of course this saying has another part, '*Ve ka'asher ani le-atzmi, ma ani?*' which means, 'But when I am being for my own self, what am I?'"

"Now I'm totally confused." I looked at my cousin in wonder.

"There are more parts to that quote, yes, it is '*Ve im lo achshav, az matai?*' which is, 'If not now, when?' Maybe you will think about that and tell me what you think when you come to visit me in Israel."

"Me in Israel? What do you mean?"

"You must come to Israel. It is not a maybe; it is something you must do!" Pesach was vehement.

"But who knows when I'll get to Israel? Maybe I'll be too scared to fly that far."

Pesach hit me over the head with his new hot-orange flying disk, which was a parting gift from me.

"You are no longer afraid, *ben-dodi*," he insisted. "Remember, we said, 'Goodbye, *pachdan*—Hello, *gever!*'"

"That's what you think," I confessed. "I have so many fears that licking one of them is no big deal."

"What does *licking* mean? I do not know that word."

"Uh, it means what you do with your tongue"—I demonstrated—"but in this case it means beating," I tried to explain.

"I don't get it! What does your tongue have to do with fear? And what is beating? I thought beating is what we do to the eggs in the morning for breakfast. Or how you hit a drum? How can it be so hard to learn English? I am here so long and I try so hard, but still I do not get it all."

"That's kind of what I meant," I tried again. "I got

over, uh, conquered one little fear, but I have a zillion ones still left to get over. Getting rid of my fears is as difficult as learning every word in English!"

"No problem for you! You finished one—you can do all." Pesach sounded almost as strong as when he'd first arrived. "And maybe we will change your name. What do you think?"

I couldn't believe it. I had finally decided that I could be a *gever* with any name, even Seymour. Maybe my cousin had less faith in me than I thought.

"I, uh, thought I was starting to do okay as myself, plain old Seymour."

"Of course, but you need a better Hebrew name— not that Shmuel stuff. Let me see, how about Shimshon?"

"What makes Shimshon better than Shmuel?"

"Shimshon is the man from the story with Delilah, you know, who was so strong, a *geebor*, a *gever*. Now you are so strong too. So shall I call you Shimshon when you come to visit me?"

"I'll have to think about that. After all, it's like you said, no one is brave all the time. Didn't Samson—that's what we call him in English—get tricked by Delilah in the end?"

"This is good! You learn things in America too!" He ducked as I grabbed the flying disk to hit him over the head. "Only joking. How you say, only kidding! But you do not have to worry about Delilah. Just keep your hair short and don't let Lari get too close."

"Lari who?" I pretended I'd never even heard the name.

"My friend's little sister, of course. Maybe we ride our bikes over there one day before I leave. Bari is coming home tomorrow for holidays."

I'd nearly forgotten the holidays. In a couple of days, we'll be celebrating the Jewish New Year. It's in the fall, because the Jewish calendar works according to the moon. I'm glad; it gives me two chances to make New Year's resolutions, and I still need plenty of resolutions.

Pesach is coming to temple with us even though he has no suit or sports jacket or anything and refuses to borrow one. He doesn't even have dress shoes. The most he agreed to was a white shirt of my father's, which sort of swims on him.

"Don't worry, *ben-dodi*, I will look like myself, an Israeli, and I will not be embarrassed. You will not want to be seen with me maybe?"

"Oh, no, if you don't care, I don't care. I can't quite picture you in a suit anyway." That's true. I can't imagine him in a suit at all. But he'll certainly stand out in the crowd. I'm sure that no one else will be there in funny brown leather sandals.

Somehow that doesn't bother me right now—nothing bothers me. This is the beginning of a new year, all right. Now that I've learned how to ride a bike, who knows what I can do next? Maybe I'll find a great article that will give me advice on how to get over a whole bunch of fears at once. Boy, that would save me a lot of time and effort.

Maybe Pesach and I will really take a bike ride together over to Lari's house. Lari and I actually talk to each other now. She says things like "Hi, how are you?" and I answer in almost complete sentences, like "Fine, and you?" Once she even called my house to ask for my help with an extra-credit math problem. And I managed to get out some words over the telephone, though I did have an awful lot of "uh, sure, uh, uh, uh"s. So maybe we'll do that, Pesach and I, casually ride by on our bikes.

I'm still running with Ted, though I don't think I'm ready for a marathon. So maybe I won't become an incredible athlete. But now that I, Seymour J. Goldfarb, can ride a bike, anything is possible. Well, almost anything—I am definitely not ready to get on another boat, in the near future or maybe ever. And I'm not sure I'm even ready to think about sleepaway camp yet, although my computer camp was so awful—how much worse could sleepaway be? Maybe I do have some of Pesach's genes, though definitely not the ones that enjoy parachuting.

I can't believe he's leaving. And I can't remember what life was like before he came. Will I ever work up the guts to go to Israel? Who knows? With the New Year and the new me, strange and wonderful things might really happen. Maybe that's what Pesach's famous quote means: *"If not now, when?"* I'll have to think about that.